W9-BZG-029

DRI

DRIFTER

•

Karl Lassiter

AVALON BOOKS
NEW YORK

Published by Thomas Bouregy & Co., Inc.
160 Madison Avenue, New York, NY 10016

Library of Congress Cataloging-in-Publication Data

Lassiter, Karl.
    Drifter / Karl Lassiter.
        p. cm.
    ISBN 978-0-8034-9940-9 (hard cover: acid-free paper)
    1. Cowboys—Fiction. 2. Wyoming—Fiction. I. Title.

    PS3572.A714D75   2009
    813'.54—dc22   2008031618
PRINTED IN THE UNITED STATES OF AMERICA
ON ACID-FREE PAPER
BY HADDON CRAFTSMEN, BLOOMSBURG, PENNSYLVANIA

b18495618

For Scott & Pat,
the best of friends along any trail.

Chapter One

The rattling Union Pacific freight car tossed John Allen around so much he couldn't sleep any longer. He sat up and stretched aching arms and legs, then shivered a mite from the cold wind whistling through the cracks in the boxcar walls. John rubbed his eyes and stood, knowing it was still dark outside. He had ridden the rails long enough from Kansas to appreciate the slow movement of day to night and back and how it seeped through to the cargo-laden interior.

John's medium height was almost too tall for the overhang of crates in the car. The car was laden with merchandise destined for Cheyenne City, or so said the labels. John yawned widely, then slipped his strong fingers around the heavy door. He tugged hard, his muscles straining. The door barely budged. When the train

1

made a sweeping curve he was thrown to one side. He quickly regained his balance and returned to his work. John worked the door open enough to find what barred his way out.

A thin wire and lead slug clamped hard with the Union Pacific seal fastened the door. Try as he might, John couldn't open the door far enough to squeeze through. It didn't help that he hadn't eaten in almost a day since sneaking into the car. He stopped trying. Breaking the seal would only alert railroad detectives that they had carried an unwanted, nonpaying passenger on their railroad.

Finding a loose plank in the floor gave him the chance to slide out. John peered at the ground racing past and almost lost his nerve. Swallowing hard, he knew this was his best chance to leave. With the cinders kicking up from the road bed and the sparks flying off spinning steel wheels only inches from his face, he made his way on the network of rods until he reached the pin connector at the front of the car. John grinned broadly. His luck still held.

He had been lucky jumping the train back in Kansas, and now he was lucky that the last passenger car was so close. It saved him having to jump from car to car and risk falling off in the darkness. Pulling himself onto the platform, he peered cautiously inside at the paying passengers.

Dim gaslights showed dozing men—and no conductor who might ask to see a ticket he didn't have. Opening the door, John slipped in and dropped into the first seat next to a man with a tall black Stetson pulled low over his eyes.

"You ridin' the rails?" came the drawled question. John jumped. He had thought the man was asleep.

"I'm taking Mr. Greeley's advice and coming west," John admitted. "I know Mr. Greeley was only quoting some newspaper man in Indiana back when he said it, but I read the whole of Mr. Greeley's piece and want to do my share."

"And you're coming to grow with the country without a nickel to your name." The man pushed his hat back and studied John carefully. Dark eyes bored into him. John never flinched. If anything, he studied the man even harder than he was being studied.

"You're a cowboy?" John had never talked to anyone making their living punching cattle but he had read about them. That, in part, drew him to Wyoming.

"I am," the man said, shoving out a paw of a hand to shake. "Name's Ben Norton. My friends call me Carver."

John returned the iron grip with one of his own, then frowned and shook his head. "How'd you come by two last names? I've heard tell that some Englishmen go by double names but you don't have that kind of accent. You sound as if you hail from closer to Texas than to London."

Carver laughed heartily. "I'm a top cowpuncher. They call me Carver because I can 'carve' out one cow and never disturb the rest. You don't know much about where you're heading, do you?"

"I'm afraid not. I've spent my time working as a gun-smith's apprentice, then a blacksmith for four years and the past eight months I've spent down in the Nebraska coal mines." John's background was a decent, honor-able one but he felt unimportant next to a man who rode the range and herded cattle for a living.

"You don't look old enough for all that, unless you started young."

"I did. When I was fourteen my parents died of cholera," John said, the memory still stinging like a net-tle in his side. "There weren't any other relatives so I apprenticed for two years. Then I moved from St. Louis to Iowa and learned blacksmithing but that didn't suit me much."

"You're a drifter," Carver said, no sting in his words. "Like me. It doesn't pay to settle down, not when there's always something just beyond the sunrise and on the other side of the wind that's new and different."

"Don't think of myself that way, but I have moved around. I read about ranching in a dime novel and it sounded so appealing I thought I'd give it a try. And Mr. Greeley—"

"Said to go west," Carver finished for him. He shook his head. "You don't know squat about being a cow-puncher, do you?"

"I'm a quick study. And there's nothing I want to do more."

"Look around you. Point out the hombres who are real cowboys, not just greenhorns prancing around and telling folks they are the finest what ever straddled a horse." Carver lifted a hand and made a sweeping gesture encompassing the entire car. "Go on, John Allen. Show me how fast you can learn."

John didn't want to stare openly since that wasn't polite, but he carefully worked from one sleeping figure to another. When he reached one man, he burst out laughing.

"That one, the one in the fringed buckskin jacket. I reckon he's never been west of the Mississippi before this trip."

"Why?" Carver stared at John, his leathery face splitting in a wide, white grin.

"The coat he's wearing is too fine. Why, it's not got a speck of dirt on it. And he's wearing two six-shooters with carved bone handles. The bluing's not even scratched on those sidearms."

"His face. What do you read in his face?"

John slouched a mite in the seat so he could see the fringed buckskin-wearer's face better. It took him several minutes of deep thought before he understood.

"He's not suntanned, and there's a puffiness to his face lacking in some of the others."

"No wind's ever blown across his countenance," Carver said in his slow drawl. "He's flush with water. Never gone a day without a drink of long, cool water in his life. And take a good gander at his hair. All cut up neat and purty by some highfalutin' barber." Carver pushed his Stetson back to let John see how his hair had been hacked off, maybe done using a knife as he peered into a dirty mirror.

"Several of them are neatly dressed. That one, for instance, but he has the hardness you attribute to being outdoors."

Carver nodded. "That one dressed all in black is a gambler. Stay clear of him, boy. He'll steal every cent you have and might not even leave you your boots."

"I don't bet."

"Good. Not that it matters. The way that tinhorn works ain't gambling. It's outright stealing. Him and two others work this train. One pretends to be a complete rube who loses big at three card monte. Then the second accomplice sidles up to their mark and convinces him he can beat the gambler, because he knows how he's cheating. Proves it with a hand or two. Greed flares and the mark agrees to put up a stake."

"And he loses," John said. He had watched gamblers working along the docks in St. Louis, some fresh off the big riverboats and others trying desperately to stay alive through any wile possible.

"You understand why you never get into a game, unless you know the folks."

"I've always been told to look around the table. If I can't figure out who the sucker is, it's got to be me." John was feeling comfortable talking to Carver Norton. The cowboy was long-winded but seemed affable and accommodating to an admitted greenhorn.

"That's good enough reason. Either you got a passel

of sensible friends or you've got a level head on your shoulders."

"I like to think both are true." Silence fell and John stared out the dirty window for a few minutes. The sun was poking above the horizon, giving him his first look at Wyoming not seen through a crack in a boxcar wall. The way the light shone off the tall mountains about took his breath away. The plains rose quickly into the Laramie Mountains and he saw more than scenery. He saw promise.

"Tell me about being a cowboy. I've read about it but—"

"You don't know a danged thing if all you've done is read," Carver said, the first note of irritation entering his voice since John sat down. "All you young bucks think on is shootin' and ridin' and heavy drinkin'." Carver squinted at John through one eye. "And maybe finding yourself a soiled dove on Saturday night for your amusement."

"I don't hold with fallen women," John said, sitting straighter.

"Saves you heartache and more. But you don't know anything about being a cowpuncher. Not a blamed thing."

"Tell me," John said, leaning forward, hands on his knees. His obvious eagerness lit up Carver's leathery face more than the dim gaslights in the car or the radiance from the new sun. "Tell me everything so I can learn."

"Can't learn by listening. You can only learn by *being*

a cowboy. Still, I might give you a taste of what a real puncher does." He settled his Stetson firmly around his ears and stared at John, as if deciding which story to regale him with. He smiled again, coming to a decision.

"I've ridden the range since I was fourteen, about the age you were apprenticed to fiddle with six-guns. Every spring, I go to Cheyenne City for the Wyoming Stock Growers Association meeting. The ranch owners hire their hands for the summer there. Either you got lucky or you know more than you're telling. This is the *only* time to get hired on in Wyoming."

"Lucky," John murmured. His heart pounded a trifle faster at the notion he was going smack into the middle of a cattlemen's meeting. His chances of finding work soared.

"You spend all day in the saddle riding herd, rounding up the beeves out on the range. Some of them mavericks don't have brands. You carve them from the herd, bring 'em over and put your brand on their rumps. It's hard work. Breaking broncos, riding all day, maybe riding all night, too, if the herd's itching to stampede."

"I've read about cattle stampedes."

"You've read," Carver mocked. "You can read until your eyes fall out and you'll never know the fear that claws at your gut when you hear the first thunder of a stampede. Nothing stands before a herd of cattle— except a cowboy doin' his job. You got to ride in front of a thousand tons of mindless death and turn the leaders. Men get killed if they don't know what they're doing."

"I can ride," John said. "I've got firsthand knowledge of horses, at least from shoeing them."

"Never been in the saddle, have you? You'll ache all over and beg to go back to your coal mine."

"Never!" John said hotly. "I can learn to stay in the saddle. No horse can get the best of me!"

"That's the spirit. I like you, John Allen. You've got fire, and there's an iron core to you lacking in those other bucks." Carver fumbled in his vest pocket and pulled out a large pocket watch. He popped open the lid and squinted at the face. "We got another hour before we reach Cheyenne City. Let me get some shuteye."

"Is the conductor likely to come by before then?"

"Don't fret on that account," Carver said. "He'll be busier than a cat in a mouse factory all the way to the station. Why don't you chew on this? It'll ease the noisy complaining of your belly."

John gratefully accepted the stale crackers and beef jerky Carver pulled from his outer coat pocket. He had less than fifty cents to his name and hadn't eaten since . . . he couldn't remember when. John forced himself to chew slowly and savor the salty tang of the jerky and the way the crackers bent and finally softened once in his mouth. Carver tugged at the broad brim of his Stetson and went back to sleep.

As he ate, John studied the others on the train, as Carver had suggested. He found it increasingly easy to pick out the greenhorns like himself. Their clothing was too elaborate, too new, their boots shining and their six-shooters untried. The others, the ones like Carver Norton, had a worn look to them that John found appealing.

That mien told of experience and hard times and surviving. More than surviving. It spoke of freedom.

John swallowed and let the food settle in his empty belly. He was too keyed up to sleep, as Carver was doing. He kept staring at the others, but his eyes stopped when they lit on a passenger at the far end of the car. John might have seen a prettier woman but he couldn't remember when or where. It was rude to stare but she wasn't likely to notice. She was arguing with the man sitting in the seat directly across from her.

John built wild tales about himself to tell the young woman, and then completely forget them. She was well-off, from the cut of her fine dress and the way she held her head so proudly. She was accustomed to giving orders and having people obey, yet John didn't think she seemed uppity. He wished Carver was awake. He could ask him if he knew her.

"Don't!" the woman said loudly, slapping away the man's hand as he reached for her. She repeated it when the cowboy across from her swung about and forced himself to sit beside her, pinning the young woman in the narrow seat. "Get back over there this minute!"

John didn't hear what the man said, but he got a good look at the stubble of beard and the long scar running down the side of the man's face. This unkempt passenger had no call to annoy the lady. John made his way down the swaying, rattling car's aisle to tower above the cowboy.

John had determined those in the car who rode the range and those who only showed a face as they thought a cowboy looked. What struck him most was all the greenhorns wore six-shooters while only a few of the true cowboys did.

The man annoying the pretty passenger wore a six-gun low on his right side, slung as if he was used to reaching often for the worn, sweat-stained oak handle. His thick, dark mustache drooped and gave him an evil aspect, and his eyes were tiny and set under heavy, bony ridges. The cowboy's eyebrows wiggled across his forehead like drunken caterpillars when he frowned, and John thought that was more often than not.

This was a mean-spirited man and quite likely a dangerous one. The six-gun looked well used. Very well used. But John didn't consider that when he spoke up.

"Ma'am, is there anything I can do to make the trip a little easier for you? A little quieter?" John forced himself to look from the woman's perfect face to the man next to her. The cowboy scowled even more, his brow turning into a rutted, sunbaked plain.

"It's all right," she said, agitated. Tiny spots of color on her cheeks told of her high emotion. John knew everything was not all right.

"Perhaps your companion would prefer a different seat? Back there." John jerked his thumb in the direction of the far end of the car.

"Who are you to tell me what to do?" The cowboy shot to his feet, hand resting on the butt of his six-shooter. John paid him no heed. He held his ground, refusing to be intimidated.

"It's all right, sir," the woman said loudly, her hand on the cowboy's wrist to keep him from drawing. "This is my fiancé's brother. We're almost family. The squabble doesn't amount to anything. Thank you for your consideration."

As she spoke, John heard her voice soften and fill with thanks. He considered abiding by her request and backing off. The cowboy bellowed something John didn't understand, then shoved him hard. John stumbled back, catching himself against another seat. With the rocking of the train, he almost lost his balance.

"That was uncalled for," John said. He set his feet, balled his fists and measured the distance.

"You've got no call poking your nose where it don't belong. I'll tear you up!" the cowboy yelled and came at John.

A short jab rocked the cowboy back on his heels. A second punch drove straight for his midsection. The blow staggered John as much as the cowboy. The man had a belly made of cast iron. John bobbed as the cowboy threw a wild punch. Ducking under a haymaker, John moved in and connected with two more quick jabs. Then he saw his chance and unleashed an uppercut that snapped the cowboy's head back. The man's eyes rolled up in his head, and he took a step back and fell heavily into the seat beside the woman.

She watched John, her expression unreadable.

"No one's ever knocked out Sam before," she said, almost in awe. He waited for a thank you. Instead, he felt a strong hand on his shoulder pulling him back.

"Excuse us, ma'am," Carver Norton said, dragging John back to his seat. "Sorry to have perturbed you any."

"Wait, Carver," protested John, refusing to be pushed around. His hand ached as much as if he had laid it on the tracks and let the train's engine run over it. He knew better than to hit a man on the chin, but the opportunity had been too good to pass up. "Let me—"

"Hush up and sit down," the cowpuncher said.

"He doesn't have any call to annoy that woman like he did!" John said hotly. He cradled his hand in his lap, rubbing it to erase some of the pain.

"That's no ordinary woman," Carver said.

John could agree to that.

"That's Lisa Holcroft, the daughter of Charles Holcroft, owner of the Rolling H, Wyoming's biggest spread. And she's engaged to marry Whitey Yarbrough, Mr. Holcroft's foreman."

"So?"

"So, you just knocked out Whitey's brother. Sam's got a streak of mean running through him that's a mile wide, and his older brother dotes on him. You might have just made two powerful enemies, and you haven't even reached Cheyenne City yet!"

John gazed down the aisle to where Lisa Holcroft sat. She caught his eye and favored him with a shy grin, before averting her eyes. John Allen didn't care if he had made a thousand enemies. That sincere smile was worth it.

Chapter Two

"**D**on't look back," Carver Norton cautioned. He put a strong hand on John Allen's shoulder and shoved him down the steps. "You'll be in a world of trouble if you tarry."

John knew the cowboy was right. If Sam Yarbrough didn't come hunting for him then the conductor would. The uniformed Union Pacific employee had been busy with passengers in two other cars. Now he worked his way back through the train, almost to the car where John had hitched a ride in comfort. John cast a quick look at the freight car and touched his finger to the brim of his cap in tribute. The ride had been rough and cold from Kansas, but it had brought him to Cheyenne City.

He didn't know where to look first. Although Cheyenne was like Kansas City or St. Louis or any of the other big towns he had seen, it was completely different. The smells were similar, and the buildings had the same look. But it was different. It was the West. And the people hurrying along on their business were entirely distinct from people back East. Most all the men wore high-heeled boots, their trousers tucked into the tops to show off the fancy designs tooled into the leather sides. None of those wearing boots lacked spurs, and all jingled as they walked.

"Does everyone carry a six-shooter?" John asked Carver.

"Not everyone. When you're on the range, it can be a real nuisance—and a way of savin' your own life. More 'n one rattler's come to a quick end from my shooting," the cowboy said.

"And the hats," marveled John. Carver Norton sported a black Stetson. Those in Cheyenne preferred white felt hats with broad brims, some decorated with leather bands and others with snake skin. John wondered what those magnificent hats cost and how long he would have to work to earn enough to buy one.

Carver chuckled. "You take care. Cheyenne is a good town but stay clear of the saloons and the gamblers. If you want to save up enough to buy duds like those, that is."

"Don't fret about me, Carver." John thrust out his hand. Carver took it and shook, his bone-grinding grip reassuring. John would miss him.

"You ask around about a job. The Wyoming Stock

Growers Association meeting is the place to find cattlemen willing to hire you for the season. Most all the spreads need men, even a tenderfoot like you." With this parting advice, Carver turned and sauntered off down the dusty street, dodging buggies and even a streetcar pulled by a team of lop-eared mules.

John stood stock-still, hesitating to lose himself in the bustle of a real western town. Then John admitted to himself he wanted only a last sight of Lisa Holcroft, but the woman never came down the steps of the passenger car. When the train had stopped, she must have gone forward past the conductor and out of John's life for good. Heaving a sigh, he set off to find some of the ranchers hurting for the kind of help John Allen could offer.

By sundown, John was footsore, tired and his spirits were flagging. He sat on the boardwalk outside a small bookstore and watched the traffic in the street. If anything, Cheyenne City boiled with more life after the sun sank behind the towering, snow-capped mountains than it had during the light of day. But John had found no one willing to hire him. Competition against hundreds of experienced cowpunchers didn't deter him. He knew he was a hard worker, but the skills he lacked kept the cattlemen from doing more than glancing at him.

"No luck?" came a gravelly voice. John turned and glanced over his shoulder. Carver Norton smiled broadly.

"None. At least, none of the other greenhorns was getting hired, either. That doesn't make it any easier to take."

"Come on in the Oriental with me," urged Carver. "I'll buy you a drink and a sandwich."

"I don't drink, but if they have some cider I'll be glad to accept your offer."

John followed the cowboy across the street to a large tent with sides flapping in the evening wind. Smoke billowed from inside. Everyone John saw puffed hard at a hand-rolled cigarette or brown quirlie. They worked through the crowd and leaned against a long plank of rough wood supported across two sawhorses.

Carver ordered a beer and sent the barkeep scuttling off to find some cider. John helped himself to pigs knuckles and a pickle from a large jar on the bar.

"You're looking expansive," John observed. "Does that mean you found a job?"

"Indeed, I did. The biggest spread in this section of Wyoming."

"The Rolling H?" John knew he was right from the expression on Carver's face.

"Sam Yarbrough never caught sight of me. You decked him too fast, otherwise I might have hunted forever if he mentioned it to his boss. Charles Holcroft hired me on the spot at thirty-five dollars a month." Seeing the amount meant nothing to John, Carver added, "Those are top hand wages. Most cowboys are lucky to see thirty a month."

John accepted the cider from the bartender and gratefully sipped at it after Carver paid. Then he set to eating a sandwich piled with meat. The crackers and jerky had been all he'd eaten in two days. John tried not to stuff too much into his mouth, but the food sat well with him.

"Much obliged," John said, wiping his mouth after wolfing down the sandwich. "My stomach thinks my throat's been on vacation too long."

"I know how it can be." Carver sipped at his beer, but his eyes were fixed across the tent on a man sitting alone at a wobbly table. "And I can spot folks hurtin' for company. Why don't you go over and introduce yourself to that gent?"

"Why him?" John saw any number of other men in the room he'd rather strike up an acquaintance with.

"That's Warner Kincaid, and he owns the spread just to the east of the Rolling H. Can't recall what he calls it. The Flying K, I think. Word's out he needs hands something fierce."

"Why's he here and not at the Stock Growers meeting where he can find men to work for him?"

"Go ask," suggested Carver. "Go on. Can't hurt none, and you might find yourself buyin' me a drink in way of celebration. Havin' a job makes you want to sing and dance and whoop it up."

John finished his cider, hitched up his trousers, then went over to the table. Kincaid didn't notice him. John cleared his throat and got the cattleman's attention.

"Pardon me for being so bold, sir, but I heard tell you might be hiring cowboys for your spread."

"Greenhorns," grumbled Kincaid, more to himself than to John. "That's all I can afford." The tall, thin man pushed back from the table. "I might as well come to grips with it. I don't have much money, son. Is that a problem?"

"I don't have experience being a cowpuncher," John said. "I'm a good worker and learn quick."

"How have you been keeping body and soul together?" Sharp eyes fixed on John, spearing him, daring him to lie. John knew better. Men like Kincaid hated lying, and John would never walk that path with him.

"Spent almost a year as a coal miner. Before that I worked as a blacksmith."

"What? For how long?" Interest flared now.

"More 'n four years. And—"

"You any good at smithing?" Kincaid motioned for John to take the seat across the table.

"There are better," John admitted, "but not around Cheyenne. I'm looking for a job as a cowboy."

"I can get cowboys anywhere. I need a blacksmith. Forty a month is a generous wage. Are you interested?"

"Yes, sir," John said reluctantly. "I'd prefer to work as a cowboy."

"There might be a chance. The Flying K will be shorthanded, but you'll be earning a whale of a lot more hammering metal than punching cows."

"That doesn't much matter, sir. I've got my heart set on riding the range."

"Forty a month blacksmithing," Kincaid said firmly. "I hope you take it, and I hope you're half as good as you say at working iron."

"I'm good," John said. He thought fast. Ever since he read stories of the open range and cowboys working the vast herds, John had set his sights on being a wrangler. But he needed a job and Kincaid offered a higher salary than Carver got. "I'll be pleased to accept."

"Shake on it." Kincaid's grip wavered slightly as John tightened down. A flash of pain crossed Kincaid's weathered face, then vanished. "I reckon you need a few dollars to tide you over." Kincaid fumbled in his pocket and drew out five crumpled greenbacks. "An advance on your salary. Be in front of the saloon at sunrise tomorrow for the wagon taking you up to Chugwater."

"Chugwater," John said, the name alien and wonderful to him. "I'll be there, sir. Thank you."

"If the gent you were drinking with needs a job, send him over." Kincaid pointed at Carver.

"No, sir, he has a job. He was the one who suggested I speak to you."

"Buy him a drink, then, and give him my thanks." Kincaid saw a ring of men had formed, all with the aspect of newcomers to Cheyenne City and all hunting for jobs. They had seen John talking with him and more than one had overheard the fine offer. John hastily returned to the bar.

"Order another round," John said, happier than he could remember being as he laid down one of the dollars advanced him by Kincaid. "I got a job"—his spirits sank a mite when he added—"as a blacksmith."

"There's no shame in having a proper job." Carver lifted his mug and said, "To a fine future on the frontier."

John finished his cider, took a second sandwich and a few pigs knuckles, then left to find a store. He doubted any would be open when the wagon rattled up to the Oriental Saloon to take him to Chugwater and the Flying K ranch at daybreak.

Strolling up and down the streets of Cheyenne City, John saw dozens of stores, all with doors open and eager clerks inside willing to take money from cattle owner and wrangler alike. He saw one smaller, general mercantile store that appealed to him. John went in and quickly walked up one aisle and down the other pricing what he would require. He had no good idea how far Chugwater lay from Cheyenne, but the trip would require protection from the elements.

He chose a yellow slicker and considered the variety of heavy coats offered, but his eyes fixed on the selection of tall-crowned hats available. The white felt, wide-brimmed ones the experienced cowboys wore drew him. He didn't want to bother with the leather leggings without seats—chaps he had heard one cowboy call them—until he figured out what they were for. But the hat!

"That's a real fine silver belly Stetson," spoke up the storekeeper. "A fine price on it, for a man of your caliber."

John lifted the hat and settled it squarely just above

his eyes. It fit well. And the price tag dangled in front of him. Eight dollars exceeded anything he could afford. Reluctantly he took it off and replaced it.

"I agree, a fine hat, but I'm more in need of a bandanna." He pulled a freshly ironed red one from a pile. "Let me poke around a bit more." John tallied his purchases and still had almost two dollars left to spend. Knowing it would be a spell before he saw a town as well stocked as Cheyenne again, he vowed to get what he could.

His eyes drifted across the case filled with six-guns, but he kept moving. Carver had said there were enough cowboys who didn't carry iron dangling at their sides. Even if he'd had the money, John wasn't inclined to purchase a six-shooter. He had worked on them for two years and there wasn't any mystery to them for him.

The canvas shirts, though, appealed to him. The only clothing he owned hung on his back. A change of clothing would do well, should he ever get the chance to wash up.

As John reached for a shirt to hold it up and see if it might fit, a heavy hand grabbed his wrist. He jerked away, startled to see Sam Yarbrough.

"Never thought I'd set eyes on you again, yellow belly," growled Yarbrough. "I seen you lookin' over them hoglegs. Go put one on and let's settle our differences like men. None of that fancy sucker punching like you done before."

"A sucker got punched," John said, holding his temper in check. "I'll be happy to go a few rounds with you, bare knuckled or with gloves."

"A six-shooter. Get a gun and we'll settle our squabble like men. If you've got the guts for it."

"I have no dispute with you, sir," John said coldly. "Your behavior was properly punished. I trust Miss Holcroft is well."

"Don't you go speakin' her name!" Yarbrough stepped back and pulled away a heavy canvas duster to free the six-shooter hanging at his side. "If you don't get a gun, I'll make sure everybody knows you backed down!"

"Now, Sam, don't go—" The clerk held up his hands as if he could push the man away. Yarbrough whipped out his pistol and cocked it.

John caught his breath. There was no way he could keep the cowboy from gunning down the clerk over nothing. Before he could say a word, Yarbrough began firing. The report from his Colt filled the small store.

Four shots, four cans of tomatoes drilled clean through. The white gunsmoke spread through the store, and John saw Yarbrough turning in his direction. The still-smoking muzzle came up so he could peer down the bore.

"I won't fight you. Not like that." John trembled with suppressed anger. He knew it served no purpose losing his temper, but the temptation was great as he faced Yarbrough. That he felt anger and not fear surprised him, just a little.

"You're a coward. You're nothin' but a stinkin', lily livered, belly crawlin' coward!"

John squared his broad shoulders as Yarbrough's hand twitched on the butt of his six-shooter. John waited for the bullet that would end his life.

"That's enough, Sam." A whiff of perfume and quick movement and John realized he no longer stared hard at Yarbrough. Lisa Holcroft interposed herself between the men. "You get on out to the wagon. We have a long way to travel, and the road is difficult at night."

"I can't let this drop, Miss Holcroft. He hit me when I wasn't lookin' back on the train. I got my honor to defend. And he won't strap on a gun and satisfy me!"

"Sam," she said firmly. Yarbrough backed off, glaring at John.

"You go find something you can buy and use as a backbone," Yarbrough shouted. "Next time we meet will be the last!"

John waited until Yarbrough left the store before breathing again. His lungs gusted in and out hard, and his nostrils flared at the familiar smell of gunpowder in the air. He hadn't even realized he had been holding his breath.

"I apologize for him," Lisa Holcroft said.

"There's no need for that, Miss Holcroft," John said.

"You know my name?" She seemed pleased. "How is that?"

"Your beauty is a conversation topic all around," he

said. He flushed when he realized how this might be misinterpreted. "I didn't mean that like it sounded. I've been over to the saloon, but they aren't—they don't—"

"Please, Mr. Allen, wasn't it? Don't concern yourself so. I understand, and I am flattered by your attention. Mr. Yarbrough is not usually so . . . overly protective. We have been to Kansas on ranch business, and the prolonged absence seems to have worn poorly on him."

"Don't apologize for him." John wanted to say more to the lovely woman but didn't know what topics might hold her attention. She was the daughter of a rich and powerful cattleman.

"Since you are buying equipment, may I assume you have found a job?" she asked, her bright blue eyes dancing.

"I have, ma'am, but unfortunately not as a cowboy."

"Unfortunately? Hardly. It's a hard life, lonely and dangerous."

"Some lovely blossoms flourish on the frontier. You are testament to that."

Spots of color came to Lisa Holcroft's tanned cheeks. "You are so gallant. That is refreshing, sir. Might I inquire where you have found employment?"

"With the Flying K, as a blacksmith."

"Blacksmith?" The pretty woman seemed surprised at this. "You don't have the physique of most blacksmiths I have known."

"I am sorry for that, ma'am."

It was the woman's turn to look flustered. "I didn't

mean that you are a weakling. Rather, most are burly brutes and so few are adept with compliments, as you are." She smiled brightly. Then the smile faded a little. "I must add, though, it is a pity you signed on with Mr. Kincaid."

"Why's that?" Worries flashed through John's mind of Kincaid being some terrible ogre.

"Rumors have it the Flying K is in serious financial trouble and might not survive the season."

"Gossip has a way of being wrong." John was less worried over his fledgling job than he was at keeping Lisa Holcroft talking. He inhaled some of her gentle fragrance and decided it was not perfume. It was simply the odor of soap and cleanliness. Her shining raven-dark hair fell in soft waves down her back, so fine and lovely John wanted to stroke it. He stepped back a little, worried about how he must smell to her, but Holcroft took no notice of his grubby clothing and unkempt appearance, either through good manners or long acquaintance with cowpunchers.

"I should not have said that much," she said hastily. "Please excuse me. We must get to the Rolling H. Good evening, Mr. Allen." With that, Holcroft vanished from the store in a swirl of wide, billowing skirts.

John froze to the spot for a moment, then walked to the door and watched as Yarbrough helped the woman into the wagon. They rattled off without even a glance back. John couldn't help wondering what Holcroft's fiancé was like. She deserved something far better than a man of Yarbrough's bile. Somehow, John didn't think Yarbrough's brother would be much different.

He went back to his purchases, but his mind was no longer on what he needed. John wondered if he would ever see Holcroft again.

Chapter Three

John Allen stood in front of the Oriental Saloon an hour before sunrise to be sure he didn't miss the freight wagon going to the Flying K. To his surprise, the saloon still operated at nearly full capacity. He poked his head in and sought Carver Norton but the cowpuncher was nowhere to be seen. John's belly grumbled a mite, but the barkeep hadn't put out any food for his patrons.

Touching the provender he had put aside the night before, John went back into the street. He took the food out and began munching on it. Left overnight, the food from the saloon had lost its taste, but that didn't bother John much. He had eaten worse, and this filled the space in his rumbling gut. He anticipated the day when he had enough to eat.

A half hour later, John saw a long, flatbed wagon

clattering along the street. A heavyset man with a drooping black walrus mustache drove expertly. He pushed back his tall hat with the floppy brim and called to John, "You one of the newly hired men going to the Flying K?"

"I am, sir," John said, coming over. "Who might you be?"

"Bill Diamond, foreman of Mr. Kincaid's spread." Diamond thrust out his hand. John shook it, noting how like tanned leather that fist was. There was no mistaking what Bill did for a living. He was a cowboy, born and bred. That hand had seen nothing but hemp rope slipping through it.

John introduced himself and said, "I showed up a mite early, not wanting to miss the ride."

"I don't much care how you get to the ranch, so long as you do," Bill said. He pulled a small leather pouch from his shirt pocket and drew out a book of rolling papers. John watched as the foreman expertly built a cigarette, finally lighting it with a lucifer taken from a metal tin kept in his coat pocket. Bill drew in the smoke, then let it curl blue and slow about his face. He saw John's interest and silently offered the fixings.

"No, thank you," John said quickly. "I don't smoke."

"Chew, then, if you want. I see you're a greenhorn but at least you're on time. The others Mr. Kincaid hired are late."

John started to point out it wasn't yet sunrise, but he held his own counsel. Bill seemed a pleasant enough fellow, but it never paid to irritate a new boss until he found out the man's true demeanor.

"I've been hired as blacksmith. Is there any chance you'll need me to ride the range?" He tossed his meager gear into the wagon bed and walked around to stand near the foreman puffing away up in the driver's box.

Bill laughed and it was a full, pleasant sound lacking in any mockery. "Never heard of a smith so all-fired eager to break his butt in a saddle. You're serious about wanting to ride?"

"I am, sir."

"No need to 'sir' me. Bill is a fine name. Use it."

"Yes, si—Bill." John climbed onto the wagon seat next to the foreman. "How far is it to the Flying K?"

"A good day's trip, maybe longer if these sorry excuses for draft animals balk." Bill spat in the direction of the powerful horses hitched to the wagon. He twisted on the seat when he heard men coming. He let out a groan. "What did I ever do to deserve *four* greenhorns?" Louder, so the three approaching could hear, Bill yelled, "Get into the wagon. We're heading out right now."

The three jumped to it, getting their gear into the rear of the heavily laden wagon. Whether the foreman had loaded the supplies the night before or if he had worked an hour or more before arriving to pick up his men, John didn't know. John hung on for dear life when Bill gee-hawed the team and got them moving. The sudden lurch had nearly unseated him.

"You get on back with the other three," Bill ordered. "Grab some shuteye. There won't be a minute's rest once we get to the ranch."

"Thanks," John said, meaning it. He had spent the night curled up behind an undertaker's parlor, using his brand new slicker and shirt to stay warm. All he had left of the advance given him was the fifty cents he had blown into town with, and the cheapest room he could find was a dollar a night.

John settled down atop bags of flour and struck up a conversation with the other men. All had the look of the tenderfeet he and Carver had joked about on the train. It irritated him that Warner Kincaid had hired them as cowboys and had passed him over for that chore.

"You worked many years as a wrangler?" one asked of him. John was startled by the question, then secretly pleased.

"Mr. Kincaid hired me as a blacksmith," he told the youth. John found himself thinking of the three as boys, hardly men, though he was only a year or two older. Somehow, there existed a gulf formed by experience. He had spent half his life working hard, smithing and mining, and this trio hardly seemed dry behind the ears.

"We're gonna be taught to work the herds," another spoke up. "We're each gettin' twenty a month too!" He spoke as if this was a princely sum. John refrained from mentioning a top hand got thirty-five.

And that Mr. Kincaid had hired him at forty a month!

They talked in a desultory manner until, one by one,

they dropped off to sleep. John watched the countryside ramble by, fascinated by the tall mountains and the stark beauty intermixed with the sweeping plains of lush grama grass and fragrant sage and noisily flowing rivers. Soon he tired of this and drifted to a pleasant sleep.

He awoke with a start when he realized the sun was tumbling behind the distant mountains to the west. Sleeping the day away had robbed him of any sense of where they had traveled.

"Get your sleepy heads out of the wagon. Unload our stores and put it all wherever the cook tells you. That's him standing over in the door of the chuck house." Bill swung down from the wagon and walked off, rubbing his rear after a day of sitting on the wooden wagon seat.

"Let's show 'em we can do a day's work and ask for more," John said, hefting a fifty-pound bag of beans and heading toward the cook.

"Get it inside and stash it in the far corner," the cook said. The man was nondescript save for his pale eyes. They seemed to bore right through John.

"Right away, sir."

"Dunn," barked the cook. "The name's Texas Dunn, and if you forget it, don't come back for chuck!"

"Would it be too bold a guess to ask if you hail from Texas?" John fought to keep from laughing. The cook started to bark out another order, then broke out laughing.

"At last Kincaid's hired someone with some wit. Or is that half a wit?" He took the bag from John's shoulder and strode off with it, showing no sign of strain.

John and the others quickly unloaded the wagon and stored the goods. By the time they finished, Dunn had plates of food set out on a long table running the length of the chuck house.

"Eat it or I toss it to the hogs," the cook growled. John saw the cook's bark was worse than his bite and he joshed him a little. Dunn returned the joke in kind and soon his mood lightened. After all the hands had second helpings, Dunn fixed a tin plate of his own and sank beside John.

"I'm happy to see a man like you out here," the cook said, wolfing down the beans and corn dodgers as if he had gone a week without chuck.

"How's that? No one else cracking jokes?"

"There's that," Dunn said somberly. "What with the rustlers, the Flying K is in a sorry way."

"I'd heard rumors," John said carefully, remembering that Lisa Holcroft had said that the ranch might not last the season.

He didn't get a direct answer. Dunn muttered and turned his face to his plate. Bill cleared his throat and glared at John from down the table.

"We don't talk like that. It might be true but we don't go sayin' it. Bad luck."

"If we say it, it'll come true?" John shook his head. "Better getting it out in the light of day so we can do something about it. If you have rustlers wearing you down every minute of the day, stop the outlaws."

Dunn snorted. "Wish it was that easy. The Wyoming

Stock Growers Association has posted rewards, big ones, and it ain't helped one little bit. There aren't many of the varmints, but they're bold."

"Enough to steal twenty head of horses only last week," Bill said glumly. "But there's not a heart beating among those owlhoots a bullet can't stop." He drew his six-shooter and laid it on the table. The foreman stared at his revolver for a moment and added, "Even my trusty old hogleg's not up to it."

"Why not? Let me see it." John took the .44 from the foreman and rotated the cylinder. He opened the gate and knocked out the cartridges onto the table and peered down the barrel, then into the mechanism. "I see what's wrong. If you want, I can fix it."

"I thought you were a blacksmith," Bill said.

"Am, but I also apprenticed as a gunsmith."

"Fix my pots first. The danged things are leakin' all over when I try cookin' in them," cut in Dunn.

"Cooking? This is what you call cooking? I've scraped better looking vittles from inside a chamber pot." Bill shoved his six-shooter in John's direction, clearly wanting the gun fixed before the cook got his pots mended.

"Repairing the six-shooter won't take long," John said. "It'll take me a spell to get the smithy set up to my liking, but I promise, Texas, to get to patching your pots right away."

"Who needs a bunch of worthless tenderfeets when we got ourselves an ambitious blacksmith?" crowed Dunn. Humming to himself, he scooped up the tin plates from the table and tossed them into a large wash-tub filled with soapy water. It took a few minutes of prodding, but the protesting hands left the chuck house without a third helping.

"Get yourself settled in the bunkhouse," Bill told John. "Then can you fix the old .44 for me? I feel a mite naked without it weighing me down."

"Right away," John promised. He hefted his gear from where he had piled it by the chuck house and followed the others to the bunkhouse. Forty beds stretched along the walls, but John counted fewer than half as filled. He chose one off to the side, wanting some measure of privacy even while yearning to be with the men doing the work he desired so much. As the new hands settled in, finding out who the others were and introducing themselves, John left with the foreman's pistol, hunting for the toolshed.

Finding it behind the stable, John poked around in the dark shed, and took out an oilcloth with dozens of small-ish tools wrapped tightly. He spread it flat at his feet, examined the screwdrivers and cutters, then hunkered down and got to work on the .44. The small screws on the frame required special attention, and the spring broken on the cylinder advance mechanism almost thwarted him until he turned a piece of stiff wire to replace it.

John thumbed back the hammer a few times, listening to it fall on empty chambers. The cylinder advanced easily now. He reloaded it with the shells removed at the chuck house.

"All fixed? You work miracles," Bill said, coming over to take the six-gun. The foreman spun the cylinder twice, finally getting around to cocking the revolver.

"Be careful. I reloaded it," John said, rolling the tools back into the oilcloth to keep them from rusting. "I might need to forge a new spring. That'll have to wait until I get set up in the smithy, but unless you do some heavy shooting, that pistol will serve you well for a few days."

"I trust it will." Bill stared at John for a moment, then helped him replace the tools in the shed. Once the door had closed, he asked, "Would you like me to teach you how to use a six-gun? It's all I can do since I can't pay you for the repair right away."

"Consider it part of my wages," John said, surprised at the offer. "Mr. Kincaid pays me enough."

"But? There's something you're not saying. I heard it in your voice."

"I don't rightly need to learn how to shoot. Instead, I'd like it if you gave me a chance to be a cowboy. A real one."

Bill laughed heartily. "Never in all my born days have I seen a man so single-minded about wanting to break his back with hard work. Do a good job with the blacksmithing and we'll see. I promise. If I need a spare hand out on the range and you can get away, I'll outfit you and let you see what it's really like."

"Thank you," John said sincerely.

"Get on over to the bunkhouse. It's late and I don't

allow any slackers on the Flying K. We'll be up and working hard by dawn. *By* dawn, you hear?"

"Right away. Uh, can I ask something first?"

"What is it?" The foreman's expression showed he expected a new demand on his good nature.

"Where's the outhouse? I got to go something fierce."

The foreman laughed and pointed. "Texas's food will do that to you. You'll get used to it—or die." Bill headed for the bunkhouse, shaking his head and chuckling to himself.

John hurried to find the wooden shack with the half moon carved in the door. He shooed away buzzing green-tailed horse flies and went inside to sit for a spell. As John was leaving, he heard the sound of horses moving not far off.

He got his bearings, then started in the direction of the soft voices and neighing animals. John stopped dead in his tracks when he saw the five mounted men. They had bandannas pulled up over their noses, hiding their faces. In the dim light cast by the blanket of cold Wyoming stars, John wasn't sure he could have recognized any of them even if they dropped their masks—but he knew what they were.

Running back in the direction he had come, John shouted, "Rustlers! A whole band of rustlers are riding in on us!" He slammed the bunkhouse door wide open and repeated his warning.

The cowboys in the bunkhouse stirred, groggy from

sleep. A couple grumbled at being disturbed just after they had bunked down. Others sat up but didn't move to get their boots on. The only one responding quickly was Bill Diamond. The foreman ran out, half dressed and brandishing his newly repaired six-gun.

"Stop!" the foreman cried at the riders near the corral. "Stop or I'll shoot!" He got off three rounds, but they rang out too late. The horse thieves cut the leather straps holding the corral gate shut. They yelled and whooped and spooked the horses so they ran.

"Get your mounts, saddle up and get after them!" shouted Bill to the cowboys in the bunkhouse. He fired three more shots, then the hammer fell on an empty chamber. Cursing, the foreman ran back inside, found his spare ammunition and reloaded. He threw on his coat and stuffed the remaining cartridges into his pocket. By this time the men had shaken off the lethargy of sleep and were reaching for their own six-shooters and boots.

John didn't have a gun, but he ran after the bolting horses, grabbing one's trailing hackamore and pulling it to a halt. He tethered the frightened horse and went after another. John caught a third by the time Bill stormed back outside, fire in his eye.

"There. Get on those horses John's caught for you. And don't stop riding 'til we've caught those sneaking thieves!"

John stepped away as the foreman tossed his saddle over the back of one horse, cinched it down tight and mounted. John watched the other cowboys chase after their foreman, vanishing quickly into the night hot on the trail of the rustlers.

John watched them go and felt as helpless as a babe in arms. He had been unable to stop the thieving, and now all he could do was stay behind and wonder what would become of Bill and the others.

Chapter Four

Sweat poured down John Allen's bare, broad chest as he heaved an anvil into place on a broad stone block. Venting a sigh of relief when he finally dropped it into place with a loud clanging noise that reverberated through the small shed, he used the bandanna bought in Cheyenne to keep the sweat from his eyes. He stepped back and looked around the smithy shed.

John nodded slowly in satisfaction at the equipment on all sides of him. He had worked in worse places than the Flying K's shop. The bellows needed more patches in the heat-cracked leather and the soft coal would not do to generate the hot fire required for proper metal shaping, but the tools were fairly new and the pile of scrap metal adequate for an entire season of shoeing horses.

The thought of horses made John sigh again. A cow

pony needed shoeing every six weeks—but he wouldn't be working near as hard, not with more than twenty horses stolen the night before. On his way to the shop, he had overheard Bill and Kincaid arguing. Twenty horses last night and another fifty over the past month had been rustled. That meant two hundred and eighty shoes that didn't have to be beat into shape over the black anvil. John had edged away, not wanting to eavesdrop when the owner and foreman had moved on to discussing lost cattle.

"Hundreds stolen," John muttered. His eyes went to the broken branding irons requiring his attention. Not as many irons would be applied to calves' hindquarters this season, either. The Flying K stumbled along rather than soaring like its brand.

John picked up an iron with a broken K and thrust it into the coals. He worked the bellows a few times and waited for the iron to heat. Smithing required a good sense of color. Too hot and the shape might be lost and temper gone. Too cool and iron turned brittle. He twisted the branding iron so the broken part glowed just right. Pulling it from the fire when it was red-hot, he placed it on the anvil and began hammering away, joining a piece of scrap plucked from the coals to repair the broken part.

He looked up suddenly when he felt eyes on him.

"Don't let me disturb you," said Kincaid. The ranch owner stood with his arms crossed, watching John work. "You surely do swing that hammer with authority. Reckon you are as good a blacksmith as you claimed."

"I do what I can," John said, uneasy at having the owner so intently staring at him. He had taken a considerable time getting the shop set up to suit himself. His work on repairing broken branding irons and other equipment had only started, though the sun was pushing up to its zenith.

"Bill Diamond says you were up before anyone else this morning." Kincaid looked around, nodding slowly. "Old Leggy left the place a complete shambles last year. Being disorganized is about all he did well. You've done powerful lot of work for any day setting up the shop, and here you are working on the branding irons we broke last year."

"Some rust on the ends," John said, wondering why the owner didn't let him get on with his work. "See?"

John felt as if a floodgate had been opened by holding out the branding iron for the ranch owner. Kincaid broke into a wide grin as he came over to inspect the iron.

"Reckon I'll have to tell the boys to be more careful. Do you think storing it in oil cloth would help?"

"Over the winter? Yes," John said, nodding slowly. He shoved the branding iron back into the fire and heated it back to the right color. He saw the glow in Kincaid's face, and it didn't come from the fire. "Mind if I ask you to pump the bellows a mite, sir? The coal's not getting hot enough and I have my hands full."

"Be glad to help." Kincaid set to pumping with gusto. "Don't get to help out much around the ranch anymore. I know that sounds mighty strange, son, but it's true. Bill handles most everything so I don't need to tend to matters often."

"You miss going on roundup?"

"I do!" Kincaid bent over and stared at the glowing coals. "Don't see how you work like this. I'm no expert but even I can see that the fire's not hot enough."

"That's what I was saying, sir. I need special coal from back in Cheyenne City."

"Missing the sights of the big town already, son? Cheyenne's not got anything Chugwater doesn't, but you can fetch coal along the ravine a couple miles from the ranch house. It's good, hard Wyoming coal."

"No reason not to give it a try." John continued working, the ranch owner pumping the bellows for him. John started to make a critical remark about the cool fire, then a thought occurred to him. "Where did this coal come from?"

Kincaid's eyebrows rose in surprise. "Why, it must be from the ravine. The smith I hired last season kept costs down, even if he didn't do half the work you've already finished today."

"Bill said to be on the job before sunup, and I was."

Kincaid laughed heartily. "Bill talks big, but he didn't mean that for a fact."

"I don't mind working. But I do wish the clinkers were hotter." John poked the fire and brought up a small flurry of sparks like darting fireflies. No matter how fast Kincaid pumped the bellows, the coals refused to heat to the temperature he needed. Realizing how this sounded, John looked up in surprise.

"I'm sorry, sir. I didn't mean to criticize your work. It's not often a boss comes to lend a hand, and I surely do appreciate it." John saw how fast Kincaid pumped, and how the older man's strength flagged quickly. Tall, thin Kincaid seemed weaker than John had first thought. A paleness crept under the man's weathered skin, giving him a sickly mien.

"Not used to such work. I ought to get out and see what is happening on my ranch more but it never seems like I'm up for it. Always a chore getting my worthless carcass moving. And I see your point concerning this coal. No amount of blowing is going to puff it into a white-hot clinker. Tell Bill you can go into Chugwater for that special smith's coal you were talking about." Kincaid paused and wiped the sweat from his face with a big white square of linen sporting a monogram. He tucked his fancy handkerchief back into a side pocket and looked at John, staring real hard.

"Yes, sir. What is it?"

"This coal. It's not too expensive, is it? For all the work you're doing, I don't know if I can afford much more in the way of supplies."

"Two dollars for a fifty-pound bag," John said. "That's a fair price and it would last me long enough to shoe most all the horses. Are the merchants fair in Chugwater?"

"As honest as any on the face of the earth. Tell Bill what you need. No, I will. I've got to go into Chugwater this afternoon. You can come along with me."

"Yes, sir." John studied the work still to be done, wondering if he ought to tend other chores or continue repairing the branding irons. Kincaid slapped him on the shoulder and left, grumbling to himself about being more active running the ranch. His step was faltering and his hands shook, putting a lie to how much he would be able to accomplish.

John decided to finish putting his shop into order rather than continuing the hot backbreaking labor, not because he was a slacker but because the metallurgical coal would make the work not only go faster but give a better result. He never turned out shoddy work when he could avoid it.

After a filling lunch prepared by Texas Dunn, John brought the buckboard around to wait for Kincaid. The owner and his foreman stood on the front steps of the ranch house, arguing again. John overheard only part of it.

"I'll let the other cattle growers know your concern, Bill. I'm sure they are having the same problems with rustlers."

John saw the foreman shake his head, as if he disagreed. "Don't hear about any thievin' over at the Rolling H," Diamond said.

"We'll be back by sundown," Kincaid said. "Keep a sharp watch for those varmints."

"Yes, sir." Bill shot John a look mingling anger and concern, spun and stalked off without a look back.

"Go on and drive, son," Kincaid said. "The cattle growers' meeting is at three. Reckon you can get us into Chugwater by then?"

"No reason I can't try," John said, snapping the reins and getting the buckboard moving at a sprightly pace. He tried talking to the owner about his desire to ride the range as a cowboy but Kincaid was lost in deep thought, only occasionally mumbling an answer. John saw he wasn't answering and finally gave up trying to make conversation, contenting himself with staring across the broad, rolling hills to the high mountains beyond.

Before he realized it, they drove into the small town of Chugwater. Only then did Kincaid stir, his eyes wide at their arrival.

"We made good time. Reckon I spent too much time thinking on my problems and not enough being civil. Please excuse me, son."

"That's all right, sir. I enjoyed the trip and eyeballing the mountains."

Kincaid smiled. "It's a powerful sight," he said, staring into the snow-capped, towering mountains all around. "You see to buying that coal while I'm at the meeting." Kincaid fumbled in his pocket and drew out a wad of crumbled greenbacks. Carefully peeling off four bills, he passed them to John. "Buy a hundred pounds of your coal. When we get this rustling under control, you'll have all the work you can handle."

With that, Kincaid walked off toward a large building at the far end of the street where a half dozen men were already gathered. John had seen men carrying the weight of worry on their shoulders before. His new boss was being worn down by the heavy load he carried. John tucked the bills into his shirt pocket and went hunting for a general mercantile.

He had no trouble finding one down the street. He led the horse, making sure both animal and buckboard were secure before going into the store. It took less than ten minutes for John to make his purchase; four dollars in a scrip did not go very far. He put the few pennies in change in his pocket, then lugged the two bags of metallurgical coal to the rear of the buckboard before sitting on the boardwalk to look around.

Chugwater was a small town but it held the same vitality John had noted in Cheyenne. Barely had he started drinking in the atmosphere of a town devoted to supplying those working the range around it when he spotted Kincaid and another man exit the two-story, whitewashed clapboard Masonic Lodge down the street. Heaving to his feet, John started for his boss.

The words carrying on the wind whipping off the high mountains turned him cold inside.

"I know you're a decent man, Warner, and as honest as the day is long. Hardworking and—"

"Then give me the money to tide me over, Marcus. We're lodge brothers. You know this—"

"I'm sorry, Warner. Everybody's being hurt badly by

the rustlers but you're taking it on the chin. No one else has had half their stock stolen."

"Only my horses, not the beeves," protested Kincaid.

"How do you reach the beeves without mounts? Your cowboys cannot walk during roundup."

"We have enough for them. Two or three horses for each man will turn the trick."

The man Kincaid spoke to shook his head sadly. "An outfit needs a string of horses. Four horses or more for each hand is a minimum for adequately covering your spread. You know how it goes, Warner. I cannot loan you one cent more. Business is bad because of those damned rustlers, and you're like a lightning rod for them."

"The Wyoming Stock Growers Association will cosign on the loan. I've spoken to several officers. They know how we're suffering from the cattle thieves." Kincaid's voice carried no hint of confidence, only heartsick maundering. With his slumped shoulders and quavering voice, he looked and sounded years older than his actual age.

"I'll need to speak with the entire board of directors, Warner. Don't get your spirits up, though, but I will do what I can. One lodge brother to another." The man stepped closer and they shook hands. Their fingers flew in some secret grasp which fascinated John almost as much as the men's words.

He held back, letting the man his boss had addressed as Marcus walk away quickly. Only when a reasonable time had passed did he approach Kincaid. He froze when another man came from the lodge hall. From his thinning hair and furrowed face, the man was older but didn't have Kincaid's tired look to him.

The men shook hands and the newcomer pointed after the retreating banker.

"He wouldn't give his own grandmother a red cent, Warner," the man declared. He ran a hand through a heavy fringe of unruly white hair before putting his expensive Stetson back on his head. "I know your problems. Why not accept my offer?"

"I can't," Kincaid said, shaking his head. "That's not my way."

"It'll be best in the long run," the man insisted. "It's a generous offer. You can't deny that."

"I'm not, I'm not. Ever since Ruth died, it's not been the same."

"I know. You're tired and the Flying K isn't producing up to snuff. With—"

The man bit off his words when four more cattlemen came from the lodge hall. He spoke to Kincaid in a lower voice. "I must go now. Consider the offer. It's the best you're likely to get."

"I know, and I thank you. But I can't. I promised Ruth to keep going, and I shall. I shall!"

The man slapped Kincaid on the back then went off with the others. John waited nearby, wondering how best to approach his boss. The problem was solved when Kincaid noticed him and beckoned.

"There you are, son. Glad you came by. I was just

talking with my banker. We're going to make it just fine, just fine." Kincaid forced a joviality into his words that was lacking in his bleak eyes.

"I've got the coal, sir. Ready to return to the Flying K?"

"That I am, and a fine meeting I had here too. Let me tell you all about it."

Kincaid spun what John knew to be a tall tale about the cattlemen's association lending a hand catching the rustlers and how the banker would give them money to ride out the worst of the storm.

John knew his new boss wasn't a liar, only a man desperately hoping to keep his ranch in operation one more year. For the first time John realized Carver Norton had been right. Life on the frontier posed greater risks than he had ever thought when reading his dime novels.

Chapter Five

John Allen lifted the hammer and brought it down with a loud ringing sound that echoed through the smithy and across to the corral where Bill Diamond and the others gathered. He turned the horseshoe, made a few more taps and then thrust it into the quenching water barrel. The hot shoe shook a mite and then hissed as a curling pillar of white steam rose to momentarily obscure his view. The steam vanished rapidly as he waggled the horseshoe back and forth in the air a couple of times. Only then did John hold it up and critically examine his handiwork.

"Not bad work," he muttered to himself. Conscientiously on the job all morning using the metallurgical coal bought in Chugwater, he had produced a dozen well-wrought horseshoes. Without the added heat generated by the new coal, he would have been lucky to get half this number finished and none would have been of such quality. It made little sense to make soft horseshoes that had to be replaced more often because they wore down faster.

He stretched and rubbed his aching arms. Smithing was harder work than digging coal, or so it seemed now. But John made no protest. If anything, he felt good at all he had done.

Shouts and roars of approval came from the cowpunchers hanging on the corral fence. John went to the door of his shop and stared at them with some longing. The twenty men selected their string of horses according to a formula John wasn't privy to. He thought Bill did most of the selecting but he could not be sure.

He heaved a deep sigh and wiped his filthy hands on an equally dirty rag. Then he started for the chuck house. Texas Dunn had bellowed that the noon meal was ready but few of the cowboys had taken any notice. They were too busy outfitting themselves and noisily choosing the horses that would stay with them during the summer and throughout the long roundup.

"Are you the only hungry one in the whole world?" Texas muttered when he saw John enter. "I have half a mind to throw the whole kettle out for the hogs."

"If you had half a mind, you would be doing something worthwhile other than poisoning decent men with this slop," John shot back. He and the cook exchanged a few more good-natured barbs.

"Here, take this and don't choke. I'd hate to have to throw you to pigs too. That might actually pizzen them." The cook set a plate of pork and beans alongside a heap of greens in front of him. The cornbread came a few seconds later with a dollop of fresh-churned butter the size of a silver dollar sitting on top. John found himself enjoying all the victuals he could take—and it sat well with him. He had worked up a powerful hunger in the smithy.

"I don't know how you do it, Texas. You're about the most sour man I know, yet you cook beans so sweet and good they're like a young lady's caress."

"What do you know of good food—or a filly's touch?" Texas dropped onto the bench opposite John and chowed down himself. "It's a waste of time cookin' for this bunch. All they want to do is ride them horses."

"They're afraid to leave their mounts," John said, shoveling in the food.

"Why? Rustlers? In broad daylight?"

"No. You. They don't want to end up eating their own horse for supper."

"Get on out of here," Texas said, taking a playful swipe at John.

"Not 'til I have a second helping. Got to check to be sure you haven't put old Dobbin in the pot." He laughed at the cook's expression and piled more onto his plate just as Bill sauntered into the chuck house. The foreman came over and towered above John.

"You still itchin' for a chance to be a cowpuncher?" His eyes fixed on John and bored in, taking his measure.

"I certainly am," John said, his heart pounding faster. "Is there—"

"You have to learn the ropes first," Bill said. "You're good at shoeing but the way you pussyfoot around a horse makes me think you've never been on one."

"I can ride. Not often, but I have ridden a horse," he amended somewhat sheepishly.

The foreman grinned broadly, then tapped the side of John's tin plate. "If you're done here, why not come out to the corral? We got a horse that just might suit you." Bill looked up sharply at Texas when the cook started to protest.

With a grumble, the cook turned and stalked away. John didn't have to see the man's face to know he wasn't pleased, and he thought he knew the reason. For all his irascibility, Texas was a good-hearted sort and didn't want a friend being made the butt of a joke.

John knew this was exactly what Bill was offering too. He was offering the tenderfoot the hardest bucking, most sunfishing ornery maverick in the entire remuda. And John wasn't going to deny him the pleasure of the joke. If he wanted to ride with them as a cowpuncher, he had to prove himself, no matter how hard that might be.

"I'm game," John said, pushing from the table. Texas said something more he did not understand. John called to the cook, "Save my lunch. I'll be back to finish it when I've broken this bronco!"

Bill laughed heartily and trailed John from the chuck house.

"There's the outlaw," Bill said. "I reckon you know this one's not a lady's gentled saddle horse, but then real cowboys don't ride horses without spirit."

"This one's got heart, Bill," crowed another of the hands. "He's too good for ol' John. I want to add her to my string. Please, Bill!"

"No, let me have the roan," another called. Another and still another added their demands until John knew for a fact this was the orneriest horse this side of Texas. And he didn't care.

"Take the hackamore," Bill said, pointing to the trailing rope. "You might want to put in a fiadore 'fore you toss on the saddle."

"What's that?" John circled the nervous strawberry roan, cautiously avoiding its starts and turns. He ducked down, grabbed the hackamore and inched along it until he had the horse under control.

"That's a special knot on the hackamore. It gives you more control. Let me—"

"No, Bill, step back," spoke up another cowboy. "If John there can ride the roan, it'll be his. But he ought to do it his own way, not yours." This sentiment met with general approval.

John soothed the skittish, snorting, pawing horse the best he could. He had worked around horses, shoeing enough to know their ways. But he lacked experience in the saddle. All his work had been done with both feet firmly set on the ground. He tried to gentle the horse, only to have it rear up on him.

He danced away before the pawing caught him on the leg. Working with hooves lacking shoes had made him cautious of being kicked. His apparent fright brought hoots and yells from the cowboys hanging on the corral fence like crows waiting to swoop down on a cornfield.

"Saddle up, John. Let's see you ride. Race you to Chugwater and back!" The taunts and cheers increased as he maneuvered the horse near the rails where a saddle hung. Securing the roan, John grabbed the saddle and flung it over the horse's back.

This produced a loud, angry snort and a series of crow hops as the horse tried to avoid being saddled. John got next to the roan and shoved his shoulder into the flank. This caught the horse by surprise. It found itself pinned between man and corral fence and unable to get away. John wasted no time heaving the saddle on and cinching down the belly strap.

"You're doing just fine. Now mount up," Bill called. "Let's see how you ride, John."

John wiped his hands on his jeans, then put his foot in the stirrup. The roan moved on him, forcing John to hop along awkwardly. He refused to ask any of those watching for help. He had to do this himself if he wanted to ride as their equal. Not one of the men had missed this moment. John would not, either.

He succeeded in heaving himself onto the horse's back. He grabbed the hackamore and pulled it around. And then the horse exploded as if a stick of dynamite had been placed under it. Arching its back and driving skyward, the horse sunfished in a vain attempt to throw John. He had expected the violent move and held onto the saddle pommel with both hands. He sailed up to the sun and then landed hard—and he held on!

"Yipeee!" John cried as the horse spun about, trying to throw him. He clung tenaciously, knees pressing into the animal's flanks. John had no illusion about being an expert. He wasn't so proud that he let loose with either hand for even an instant. To have done so would mean taking a high dive off the horse's arching back.

But the horse had more than one trick to unseat the unwary. John felt the saddle slipping and then he was flung through the air. He landed so hard it knocked the air from his lungs. Gasping, he tried to sit up and couldn't. Through the roar in his ears, he heard the loud laughter of the others.

Finally getting air into his tortured lungs, he sat up and wiped dirt from his face. The strawberry roan had kicked free of the saddle and was pawing hard at it, taking out its rage at being ridden for even a split second.

"You forgot to make sure the horse didn't have a belly-ful of air," Bill said. "You have to drive your knee into its gut to make it exhale. *Then* cinch up the saddle." Strong hands pulled John to his feet and shoved him in the direction of the outlaw roan. "Try it again."

And John did. He brushed off the dust and grinned

wryly as he approached the horse. The roan spun about, lowered his head and reared some more, pawing up a cloud of dirt.

"You got the better of me once," John said in a level voice, "but that'll be the last time. You're about to be ridden." He walked slowly and got close enough to scoop up the hackamore.

"That's tellin' him, John. Ride him, boy!" called one of the cowpunchers. John ignored him and concentrated only on the roan. Any distraction might prove more than dangerous. It might mean his death. John had seen a horse kick a man to death once.

He repeated the trick of pinning the horse between his body and the corral fence. This time he made sure the roan didn't hold any air in its massive body. He found he tightened the cinch another hole along the broad leather strap. And into the saddle John jumped.

John shouted as the horse surged again under him, turning and twisting and doing its best to unseat him. Jarred violently this way and that, John clung to the saddle with grim determination. He had been made the butt of the cowboys' joke once. It was time for him to turn the tables. He was going to ride this goose-rumped green outlaw or know the reason.

John heard the cowpunchers' cries turn from taunts and jeers to calls of encouragement as he held on for dear life. He quickly learned to anticipate how the roan turned and was always waiting for the sudden turn, the abrupt stop or the sunfishing. After a few minutes of violent turns that left the horse with foam-flecked sides, the roan quieted.

As it quieted, John bent low and murmured soft encouragements into its ear. Within five minutes, he trotted around the corral, in control of the once-balky horse.

John rode over to where Bill hung on the corral fence and pulled back on the hackamore to halt the roan. The horse obeyed reluctantly.

"That's about the slickest job of breaking I ever saw," Bill complimented. "And I thought you were a greenhorn. This one's yours on the roundup, if you finish your work and can join us."

"You mean it?"

"We'll see that you get another horse. Maybe old Sadie, just to give you a change of pace. Sadie's not got the spirit this one has, but she won't buck until your back teeth come loose, either."

"Thanks, Bill. What do I do now?"

"Get the horse over to the barn and curry and comb him. You might want to give him a carrot."

"Thanks," John said, meaning it. He dismounted gingerly, wary that the horse would turn on him. But the roan's fight was drained and let John lead him to the barn. John basked in the admiration of the other cowpunchers.

His fellow cowpunchers, he told himself as he went into the barn. But once inside the cool interior, John moaned softly. Every muscle in his body screamed at the strain he had placed on it, and it even hurt to draw a breath. Being a blacksmith kept his muscles hard—riding the bucking roan had pulled and stretched those muscles in ways God never intended.

It was pure agony grooming the horse, but John didn't complain. He had been promised a chance at riding the range.

Chapter Six

"You doin' anything worth a bucket of warm spit, John?" Bill Diamond's voice cut through the din of the heavy hammer smashing into a red-hot horseshoe. John jerked around, a smile crossing his face.

"Reckon I'm about done with the shoeing. Even got shoes on Arroyo," John said, putting a name on the strawberry roan. "That took a powerful lot of doing. He'd've like to have kicked me into next week."

"I watched," Bill said. The foreman came into the smithy, thumbs hooked into his belt. He wore leather chaps and a look that told John something good was going to happen. "You figure you can ride Old Sadie for a day or two? Arroyo's too much of a horse for you."

"I heard Lou tried to ride him and was tossed off a

63

few times," John said with some pride. Lou Cassidy was one of the few wranglers working on the Flying K who had more than a year's experience. John had talked with the cowpunchers and knew they all wanted the strong, spirited horse for their own but so far John was the only one to stay in the saddle longer than it took to hit the ground. Arroyo had taken a fancy to the man who had ridden him first—and that man was none other than John Allen!

"We'll get a bridle on that one before you know it."

"You mentioned me and Old Sadie. What do you want?"

"Might need some flour from Chugwater," Bill said, the gleam in his eye telling he enjoyed this joshing. "Or you could ride the fence running south toward the road."

"There's not much barbed wire in that direction," John said. Most of the Wyoming range was open. That was why the cowboys had to round up the herds and put brands on their rumps. All winter the herd had grazed the sparse grass, sometimes coming in close to the ranch house for hay stored up against blizzardy weather, but spring had scattered the herds across the open range. After birthing the calves, the cows needed to be brought in and the best of them taken to market.

Roundup!

"How'd I come to overlook that?" Bill scratched his chin, then said, "You aren't needed for riding fence. Texas didn't mention needing flour or salt. That means you can ride along with us when we brand the heifers and round up the cows with their calves. You ready for it?"

"I was born ready!" John dropped his hammer and thrust the shoe into the quenching barrel. "I have to tend the fire a few more minutes, then I can—"

"Whoa, rein back. You need to get some gear. Outfit yourself from stores. Texas will see that you've got what you need. The others already have a string of horses to use. We don't have enough mounts to go around, so it'll be just you and Old Sadie."

John knew the others had five or six horses each, switching mounts when one tired. In a day's herding, the cowboys might use all their horses once. The rustlers had taken half the Flying K's remuda and made roundup that much more difficult. A cowpuncher on a tired horse was a liability.

"I'll do what I can with Arroyo," John promised.

"No, no, the roan gets left behind. We don't have the time to break a horse on the trail."

John's spirits sank a mite. If he had only the decrepit Old Sadie under him, he wouldn't be doing much work. The mare provided slow but sure transportation and little more. Her cutting days were past. But it hardly mattered. He could borrow other horses from the string.

"We're ridin' out after Texas Dunn tries to poison us with lunch. Won't get far before sundown, but the real work starts in the morning." Bill laughed again at John's eagerness to join in such backbreaking work and left the shop.

John hardly thought of such toil as onerous. He was going to ride the range as a cowboy!

John sat astride Old Sadie and just stared at the sheer mountains still capped with linen-white winter snow. Grama grass poked up all around in thick green tufts, furnishing free feed for the roaming herds. John shifted his gaze down a little from the mountain peaks and saw the brown dots scattered around the rolling grassland and knew the work ahead of the Flying K punchers. Rounding up that widespread herd would require long hours of work. Somehow, being in the middle of Wyoming, free and able to look a hundred miles in any direction, made him feel more alive than he ever had before. He took a deep breath of the icy air and let it out slowly.

Being trapped underground in coal mines had drained his vitality. Sitting in the saddle, wind blowing through his hair and sun burning his face to leather, made him come alive.

"There's the first bunch, men," the foreman called. The Flying K cowpunchers let out a whoop and started down a long slope, their spare horses trailing behind. John felt a pang of envy. When they reached the tableland five hundred feet lower, they would set up camp, switch horses and get to work. All he would do was follow along at Old Sadie's stately pace.

"You ready, John?" Bill asked.

"Reckon I am." It hadn't taken long for him to realize the foreman wanted him on the roundup to repair the branding irons, not to cut cattle and brand them. "Any chance you can use me to—"

"John, we've been over this ground before. You watch how they work. Even the greenhorns ride better than you."

John said nothing about riding Arroyo. The foreman knew that and had made his decision. Feeling happy simply to be along, John nodded silently and urged Old Sadie down the slope. If he couldn't ride with the others, he would show Bill how useful he could be in camp and with the irons.

Setting up camp proved simple. They dumped their gear, switched mounts and rode out straight away.

"Ride with me," Bill said in such a way that John knew it wasn't a request as much as it was an order. The foreman didn't want him getting into trouble.

"I've got what I need for working the irons," John told Bill.

"Good. You watch real close and learn what it means to carve a calf."

The mention of "carving" reminded John of the cowpoke he had met on the train. He wondered how Carver Norton fared on the Rolling H. The land stretched as far as he could see and any unbranded cow was fair game. Somehow, John thought it wouldn't be much of a contest pitting Bill against Carver Norton—the top hand riding for Charles Holcroft's spread would come out the winner every time. John knew Bill was a good man, but something about Carver Norton shouted know-how when it came to cattle.

He trotted along after the others as they fanned out to circle small knots of cattle. Slowly, over the course of the afternoon, they gathered a sizable herd. With the foreman, John rode through the cattle spotting brands. More than a few sported the Rolling H brand and Bill used the end of his lariat to whack their rear ends and get them out of the herd.

"No need to tend to another man's cattle," Bill told him. "Fact is, Charles Holcroft has ten times as many cows as Mr. Kincaid. He ought to be giving us a helping hand."

He let out a whoop and raced off, leaving John to trail behind. When John saw the reason, a grin split his face. He urged his tired horse forward as he watched Bill expertly guide his pony between an unbranded calf and its mother. The cow lowed and then allowed Bill to carve it toward a draw where the others had started a fire. Three branding irons heated in anticipation of this single calf.

"Here she comes, boys. Get ready for her," Bill called. He expertly loosened the lariat and formed a loop. Two quick spins and he had it over the calf's head.

His horse immediately dug in its hooves and brought the cow up short, complaining bitterly at such treatment. Bill hit the ground running and followed the rope. John wasn't quite sure what the foreman did but the calf found itself upended and dumped on its side. Three quick turns of rawhide cord secured its feet.

"Get that iron over here pronto. This one's too feisty to hold long."

John rode closer, watching as the foreman took the heated iron and placed it on the calf's hindquarters. A hiss, a loud cry, more of fear than pain, and a smell of singed hair rose to mingle with the juniper and sage in the air.

"That'll do it," Bill said, yanking the rawhide cord free. The calf struggled to its feet and raced back to its mama. But the cowboys didn't have a chance to admire their foreman's handiwork. Another wrangler herded over a calf and the branding was repeated. John watched for a spell, then got to work himself when one branding iron, heated too many times, cracked.

"Can't put a sloppy brand on," Bill told him. "Too many times a dispute can arise over the exact brand."

"What's to keep you from finding a cow with another brand and then putting the Flying K on the calf?"

"Nothing," Bill said. "And that's how range wars start. We work together pretty well most of the time, but sometimes men get greedy. We don't have that problem. Mr. Holcroft runs most of the beeves in these parts and he is an honorable man."

"I remember last year," another hand piped up. "We had a dispute over a calf—might have been his, might have been Mr. Kincaid's. We talked it over and Whitey decided to let us brand it. Good animal. Fetched a goodly price, I imagine."

"Whitey Yarbrough?" John sucked in his breath as he asked.

"Mr. Holcroft's foreman. You know Whitey? Good man, that one," said the wrangler. John caught the expression on Bill's face from the corner of his eye. The Flying K foreman didn't seem as inclined to share that opinion. John asked.

"Whitey's a decent sort," Bill said reluctantly. "Never found him to be anything but honest, but—"

"What about his brother?" John asked. "I ran into Sam Yarbrough on the train coming into Cheyenne."

"Sam's a hothead but he's harmless enough. He talks big but he doesn't have the grit in his gizzard to follow up on it. Let's not stand around jawing. Get that calf before it slips free. And you, Garson, there's a half dozen unbranded calves left in that knot over there. Get 'em all. What do you think Mr. Kincaid's paying you for?"

John worked silently repairing the branding iron and then found another that had cracked. He heated it and beat it back into shape before discovering he was also responsible for tending the men's tack. One wrangler had blown a stirrup. John worked it back until it was usable. Then he found another had torn loose the fender on his stirrup, riding too close to a thorn bush.

The heat built, even this far up in the mountains, and sweat poured off John as he toiled. But he never complained. If anything, he knew he had the easy job fixing the wranglers' gear rather than riding and cutting. First-hand he saw why so many of them wore the leather pants without rears—chaps. Without leg protection, the cowboys would have been ripped to bloody ribbons by the end of the day chasing calves through the tough underbrush.

As the sun dipped low in the west, Bill called, "Get the herd moving. We can set night herd when we get them into that ravine below our campsite."

The men, mostly new at herding so many cattle, slowly moved the herd of almost two hundred beeves sporting new and old Flying K brands. John rode at the rear of the herd, watching how the cowboys kept the herd together and moving in the direction desired. He realized his notion of simply staying in the saddle and being a cowboy had been naive. Even the tenderfeet among the Flying K crew showed skill both riding and roping. John found his rear end complaining after only a few hours in Old Sadie's saddle.

"Chow!" came Texas Dunn's loud cry. "I've been burnin' the beans special for you boys all afternoon."

"And I thought it was a range fire," Bill grumbled. He dismounted and brushed dust off his clothing.

"What do I do?" John asked.

"We ought to let the greenhorn ride night herd," suggested one of the older hands. "John's so all-fired eager to be a cowpoke, it'd be good schooling for him."

"Be glad to. All I need do is ride around and keep

them in one place?" John was enthusiastic that another had suggested him for the chore.

"Don't let them gull you into thinking night herd is easier. It's not," Bill said. "It's lonely and you got to sing to the cattle. If you don't, they get restless and think on running."

"The way John sings," Texas said, "he'd run 'em all off. I heard him when he was taking a bath the other day."

John swapped insults with the men until they gathered around to eat. Then he realized Bill hadn't been lying about night herd. He put his most experienced riders out to keep the herd quiet.

"Why's that?" John asked the cook.

Texas started to lie, then saw John was sincere in his question. "Ever see a stampede? No, of course, you haven't. It's deadly when it happens. Those critters ain't got the sense God gave a goose. The smallest noise and off they go. Think of that happening in the dark."

"They'd kill themselves, running over the edge of an arroyo or into a canyon."

"Worse," Texas allowed. "They'd kill the men working the herd. Best to keep the cows quiet and calm. Takes a strong hand and a knowing one to do that. Before this roundup's over, most all those gents will have ridden night herd."

"But the men out there have been working as hard as any of us," John said. His voice trailed off when he realized the long hours spent in the saddle didn't end at sundown.

"Four, five hours of riding night herd will put them in a fine mood. Not even my fine coffee will perk them up."

"Fine coffee?" John spat some onto the ground. "Lookee there. It's killing the ants!"

Texas said something uncomplimentary about whippersnappers not appreciating his victuals, then set to cleaning his pots. John found a spot to unroll his blanket and stretched out, watching the herringbone pattern of high clouds catching the setting sun. They shifted from white to pink and orange and then turned frosty as the sun left the Wyoming mountains for another day.

John tried to sleep but found himself too keyed up. He stood and walked around the camp. A few of the wranglers played harmonicas or tended to repairing their gear. He found Bill sitting and staring into the campfire.

"What can I do for you, John?" The foreman looked up, his face drawn.

"You're not looking too happy about the day's work. Is anything wrong?"

"We ought to have rounded up twice the cattle we did. Calves aren't as plentiful as last year, either. Mr. Kincaid's not going to like it unless we find a whole lot more in the next few weeks."

"It's only the first day," John pointed out. "There's a load of time."

"Maybe so," Bill said, still distant. "You mean it when you said you wouldn't mind riding night herd?"

"No! I'd be glad to!"

"I'm going to let you take the hour just before dawn.

That'll give some of the seasoned hands an extra hour's sleep and not much happens then. By the time the herd gets restive, the whole crew will be up and able to handle anything going on."

John didn't care about the reason he was given the last shift. Being allowed to work the herd was fine with him. "I won't disappoint you, Bill."

"I know you won't. The Flying K would be in better shape if we had a dozen more like you. Get some sleep and relieve Lou Cassidy around 4 A.M. He'll appreciate the rest since he's been doing the work of two men." Bill stretched out on his own bedroll and closed his eyes. But John realized the foreman wasn't sleeping.

He went back to his own blanket and lay wide-eyed for hours, too excited at his opportunity to sleep. Around three in the morning, John gave up trying to sleep and rolled his blanket. He wouldn't ride alone. He could find whoever rode night herd on this shift and keep him company and maybe learn a trick or two along the way.

"There, there," John said, soothing Old Sadie. The ancient mare had thought her night herd days were past and complained when she found it wasn't so. John saddled her, making certain he had cinched the saddle down tight enough not to slip.

He put his heels to the animal's flanks and eased her into the night. The last dim glow of embers faded from his sight and he found himself wrapped in cold mountain air. Following the lowing of the cattle, he made his way to the herd. In the distance, he saw the faint silhouette of a rider working to get a half dozen cattle back into the main drove.

Riding slowly, the cattle only yards away and restive at his passage, John worked his way toward the distant rider. As he neared, he frowned. He had thought the wrangler worked the cattle into the herd. Instead, it appeared he cut them from the herd.

When four more dark figures appeared to aid their partner, John went cold inside.

Rustlers!

Chapter Seven

John stood in the stirrups, Old Sadie moving restlessly under him. He tried to make out the features of the men working the herd—his herd! Bill Diamond had put him riding the Flying K cattle, and it was his duty to keep them safe. He turned and saw another cluster of riders joining the first.

"Ten men, maybe more," he said softly, patting Old Sadie's neck to keep the horse calm. John didn't wear a six–shooter at his side, as some of the others did. And there wasn't a rifle shoved into the sheath on his saddle. He had seen no reason to ask Texas for one. Now he was sorry he hadn't. All he had to fight off the rustlers was a single coil of rope dangling from the saddle. The more he thought on it, the less likely he was to accomplish anything more than ending up dead if he tried to lasso them.

"Get 'em moving," came the faint words drifting on the still night air. The rustlers moved the cattle they had stolen from the rest of the herd. If they got away with them, it would take only a few hours before a new brand rode on their hips, showing the world these cattle belonged to some other outfit.

"Wait up," another rustler called and then pointed. "There's a rider over yonder." Heads turned and John knew they had spotted him.

When a tongue of flame leaped into the night, he knew he had been fired at. The familiar sound of a rifle report came a split second later, along with the whine of lead sailing past his head. The bullet missed by a wide margin, but the sound startled Old Sadie. Inexperienced, John fought to keep the horse from bolting.

A second shot came his way, more to keep him at bay than to injure him. He regained control of the horse and turned her face toward the cowboys' camp. He put his heels into her sides and started yelling.

"Rustlers! They're making off with the herd! Rustlers!"

He galloped into camp, bringing the others upright out of a sound sleep.

"What's wrong, John?" Bill called. He rubbed his eyes, still more asleep than awake. The hands always joked about what a sound sleeper the foreman was and how he would sleep through a tornado. There was a powerful storm brewing, but it had nothing to do with cyclones.

"Rustlers. They're getting away with part of the herd. Back that way." John pointed over his shoulder in the direction taken by the cattle thieves. Already Bill and the others struggled to pull on boots and get their six-guns.

He wheeled Old Sadie about and waited impatiently for the others. If he had been armed he might have stopped the rustlers. Then good sense pushed out the panic. He wouldn't have stood a chance against ten armed and dangerous men. They undoubtedly all packed six-shooters. Even if he had ridden up to them and hit one with every shot, four of them would have remained to return fire.

"Come on!" he urged. "Get moving!"

When he saw Bill and two others throwing saddles onto their mounts, John lit out again. He might not stop the varmints from stealing the Flying K cattle but he could lead the way for the others. Bill looked to be handy with his pistol. The others must be, also. He wished again that he had a rifle now.

Fire pulsed through his veins as he rode hard after the rustlers. He saw them herding the stolen cattle down a ravine and took to the high ground, intending to cut them off. More gunfire came his way, but with Bill and the others backing him up John knew no fear. He lowered his head and kept Old Sadie pounding along as fast as her hooves could take her.

The night air filled with lead. John kept his head down and let the rest of the cowboys begin firing. Then he feared his own outfit might ventilate him from the way they sprayed bullets around without having a decent target in their sights.

"Hold up, men," Bill called. "Don't go getting too antsy. Which way did they go, John?"

John trotted back and pointed. "They drove the cattle that way, into the canyon."

"Finding them is going to get mighty hard," the foreman said. "That's Scissors Canyon. For every canyon branching to the north, there's two going south."

John watched as Bill made up his mind. Chasing the outlaws would be risky in the dark, but Warner Kincaid couldn't afford to lose so many cattle.

"You hang back, John," Bill ordered. "The rest of you, get ready for a fight. We can overtake them since they have to drive the herd. When we catch up, it'll be a fight to remember!"

John heard murmurs among the men showing they weren't happy about chasing rustlers into the dark, winding canyon. To their credit, not a one hung back. All rode forward with their foreman leading the way. John trailed behind, thinking he could ask one of the others for a rifle or handgun. Before he could find anyone carrying a spare firearm, the night lit up with foot-long tongues of orange flame.

"We got 'em, boys! There they are!" Bill's six-shooter flared along with the others from the Flying K. Their headlong assault slowed as they fired ahead into the canyon. All John could do was hang back and wait.

He patted Old Sadie's neck to gentle her, but the horse

kept sidestepping and shying away from the loud noise. John squinted as the muzzle flashes grew in intensity— but they all came from the Flying K side. He started to call out to Bill that something was wrong when the fore- man let out a yell and charged ahead into the darkness.

"We got 'em on the run. Get them, get back the cattle!"

John started to follow when he heard sounds echoing down a side canyon. As his attention turned that way, a bullet winged toward him. He felt its hot passage frac- tions of an inch from his cheek. He jerked away instinc- tively, then took in what had actually happened during the fight. The rustlers had sent a man or two along the main canyon floor to lure Bill and the others while the other outlaws had driven the cattle down this side canyon.

More lead came his way, but John knew retreat would only earn him a bullet in the back.

"Here they are, men!" John cried at the top of his lungs. "We got 'em dead to rights. They're in the side canyon!" He ducked a couple more slugs winging his way, then called out, "Surrender! We got you surrounded. You can't get away!" He made as much noise as he could, forcing Old Sadie to rear and neigh loudly. Her hooves crashed into rock and sent sparks flying off her horse- shoes. All the while, Bill whooped and hollered, trying to sound like a dozen different cowboys.

The bluff worked. He saw three men separate from the herd and ride off, their horses kicking up dust high in the still night air. Another rustler cursed and even fired at the fleeing men.

"He's spooking us. There's no one else. We lured them away. Keep the cattle moving. I'll take care of him."

A dozen tongues of brilliant flame leaped outward in John's direction. The deeper report told him the outlaw had opened fire using a rifle. Behind him came the others from the Flying K, realizing their error and hearing the new gunfire. John rode on, causing the cattle to react. They found a leader and a small stampede began, scattering the remaining rustlers.

"Get them," John called to the Flying K cowboys, turning to head after the three who had already fled. He forgot he was unarmed. Caught up in the heat of pursuit, he left the stolen cattle and the rustlers caught in a lilliputian stampede for Bill.

Old Sadie began to flag quickly, her sides heaving and flecked with lather. The heat of the moment also passed John and he reined back, aware of the folly in pursuing armed desperadoes. Beginning to stumble, the horse could not go on.

"There, there, we did our job. We chased them off," John said, patting the horse's neck. He dropped to the ground to give the mare added rest. "We saved the Flying K having more than a few head of cattle stolen from under our noses." John knew every head mattered to Kincaid, even if they weren't going to make expenses. Still, the roundup had just begun. More calves might be found in higher pastures and turn the season into a profitable one.

If nothing else, John had just earned his pay. Not a

single head of cattle would sell for less than forty dollars. The four months he would be hired on at the Flying K had been covered saving the dozen or more cattle being stolen.

"Let's head on back and see how Bill and the others fared," John said soothingly to Old Sadie. He patted the horse's neck, then tugged on the reins and got the horse reluctantly started back to camp. For her part, she would be more than content to stand here for the rest of the night and go to sleep.

John hadn't gone ten paces when new gunfire echoed through the night. These sharp reports came louder, as if amplified. He turned back and tried to make out the rugged terrain. An especially dark slash in the mountains might mark a canyon mouth—and now gunshots came from that direction. And with it came the sound of hooves pounding like frantic drum beats.

Another fusillade ended with a loud cry of pain. John forze, not knowing what to do. The Flying K crew wasn't the only outfit working this range. If the rustlers had come upon someone else, they would open fire without hesitation. Or had they turned against one of their own?

Torn by indecision, John looked from what must be a canyon back in the direction of the herd and the safety of the Flying K camp.

"Sorry," he told his horse. John swung into the saddle and started toward the dark cut in the mountain wall. Old Sadie tried to balk but John applied firm pressure with his knees and used the reins lightly to get the horse moving. He wondered what sort of fool he was, riding into sure danger like this.

But he had to see what had happened. The gunfire and moans of someone being injured echoed too strongly in his head to ignore. He picked his way carefully across the increasingly rocky ground until he found a well-ridden path leading into the canyon.

High walls crept closer until his shoulders brushed the cold rock, threatening to crush him if he rode too much farther. John swallowed his fear and worked his way along the trail. Like giant sentinels the rocky walls soared on either side and engulfed him. What light there had been from the stars now dimmed, shut off by solid rock. Only a thin ribbon of starlight directly above lit his path.

He tilted his head to one side and strained to hear any sound, no matter how faint. From deep in the canyon came the receding thunder of horses' hooves. But no new gunfire warned him away. John glanced over his shoulder and knew he ought to fetch Bill and the others.

"They've got their hands full tending the herd," he said aloud, as if this would chase away the fear still stalking him. "And the rustlers. They probably have them penned up now, waiting to take them into the marshal's office in Chugwater."

John didn't even know if the small town could afford a town marshal, but there had to be lawmen roving the countryside. A sheriff enforced the laws in the county. A posse deputized to put an end to the rustling must be on patrol. And hadn't Mr. Kincaid said the cattle crowers association had a reward out on the rustlers' heads? Whoever represented the law, the rustlers Bill had caught would end up in their custody.

The sloping rock walls cut off more starlight, plunging the canyon floor into almost complete darkness. John could have ridden past an entire gang of outlaws and never known. He listened harder and relied more on Old Sadie's acute sense to warn him of danger. Although the mare protested any movement, she didn't shy from riding deeper into the canyon.

When he heard a man's moans of pain, John knew there was no turning back now. He urged Old Sadie on, worrying about what—and who—he might find in the narrow canyon.

Chapter Eight

A loud cry of pain sounded, then died slowly. John Allen knew the injured man had to be in a bad way from that pitiful sound. He dismounted and warily crept forward on foot. He thought the rustlers had long since ridden on, but he dared not take the chance by bulling his way into a situation that might turn deadly in a heart-beat. An unarmed man against armed outlaws stood no chance.

He almost stumbled over the man lying sprawled on his face in the dirt trail. The dark form stirred slightly, coughed wetly and then fell silent. Ominously silent. John dropped the reins of his horse and knelt to see if the wounded man still lived.

He rolled him over and recoiled at the sight of blood on the man's chest. A bullet had cut clean through his shirt and the flesh underneath. John put his fingertips to the man's chest and felt a distant, thready beating.

"You're one tough hombre," John said. "You're going to be all right now that I've found you." He spoke as much to keep his own spirits up as to encourage the man. John knew little about gunshot wounds but this one looked bad.

He was rewarded by the flutter of eyelids. The man struggled to focus his eyes as he looked up. A shaky hand tried to touch him. John caught the man's thick wrist and forced him to lie still.

"Don't exert yourself. Save your strength. I've got to get you back where a doctor can patch you up."

"Rustlers," the man croaked out between dried lips. "I came on three of the sidewinders. They plugged me." His hand moved to the wound on his chest. John saw a trickle of blood oozing from the wound. Dead men don't bleed.

"I know. They were stealing beeves from the Flying K herd. I chased them into this canyon and . . ." In a way, John was responsible for the man's condition. If he hadn't spooked the outlaws, they wouldn't have come this way and bushwhacked an innocent man. Then he realized the outlaws were likely to shoot anyone at any time for whatever reason—they were pure poison. He had kept them from stealing his boss' cattle. He was not responsible for this man's injury.

The owlhoot pulling the trigger was.

The wounded man tried to say something more but

the words faded to a confused whisper. John stared at him, thinking he had seen him before. It slowly dawned on him that this was the man Kincaid had spoken to after his banker had turned down his request for a loan. John wasn't sure what had been said, but it seemed the offer had been to buy the Flying K.

An offer Kincaid had turned down.

"Rolling H," the man forced between his white, pinched lips. "Get me there."

"It's about the nearest, I reckon," John said. "I'll fetch my foreman and we'll take good care of you." The man reached out with a surprisingly strong grip and held his arm.

"Thank you," was all he said before he sank back, closed his eyes and passed out.

John stood and turned, then tensed when he heard the echoing of horses coming up the canyon. If three rustlers had come this way, maybe the rest had escaped and taken to this trail. They might have their hideout somewhere deeper in the canyon. John turned back to the wounded man, wondering how he could hide him. Moving a wounded man was dangerous, and unconscious the man presented a real chore to move to safety.

Then a familiar voice called out. "John! That you? You all right?"

"Bill, over here. I found a man gunned down by the rustlers. He's hurt something fierce."

Bill, Lou Cassidy and two more Flying K wranglers rode up. The foreman dismounted and came running.

"We chased 'em off. I wish we could have caught them, but they're slipperier than greased garter snakes." He stared down at the fallen man and let out a low whistle. "He's hurt real bad." Over his shoulder, the foreman called, "One of you go fetch Texas. Have him empty the chuck wagon and bring it to the mouth of the canyon. We got to get a wounded man over to the Rolling H pronto!"

"I don't know much about doctoring, but he's bad off. Is he going to live?"

"He's tough," Bill said. "One of the old pioneers in these parts. He'll make it." Bill drew John away from the fallen man and said, "I'm going to let everyone know what you did tonight. You saved the Flying K from a big loss and proved your mettle. They might have gotten clean away with thirty or more cattle if you hadn't alerted us. Thanks." Bill thrust out his hand.

John took it and shook.

"Now can I ride herd?"

Bill stared at him for a moment, then broke out laughing. "If that's all the reward you want, Mr. Kincaid's getting one fine deal. We'll try not to break too many irons or need more shoes for you to bend on that hot forge of yours. And Texas can let his pots leak. We've got ourselves a new cowpuncher!"

John broke into a smile, then sobered when he realized the work was far from over. He pointed to the man and asked, "Want me to see him over to the Rolling H?"

"You and Texas can handle him," Bill said, nodding.

"We've got a roundup to conduct. I want to get as much work done as possible before you get back. You know how greenhorns slow up a job." He slapped John on the back, smiled broadly and called the others over. They gingerly carried the injured man down the trail and waited at the canyon mouth for Texas to drive up in the wagon an hour after dawn.

"I used some of the blankets to make a bed for him. He won't bleed much on 'em, I reckon," Texas said, frowning at the way the cowboys put the unconscious man in the wagon bed. "And remind me never to let you galoots tend me if I fall sick. You'd be the death of me. You're handlin' him like he was a sack of potatoes."

"Sick, you? Never happen, Texas," John said. "You're about the toughest gent west of the Mississippi." John saw how the cook puffed up at this compliment. "You have to be to survive your own cooking this long."

"Ingrate," Texas grumbled. He piled into the driver's box and snapped the reins. John jumped up beside him, working to fasten Old Sadie's reins to the brake handle beside him. They rolled across high pasture land until they came to a twin-rutted road.

By now the sun had climbed. John estimated that it was almost eleven o'clock. He yawned widely and stretched aching muscles, but he didn't feel the least bit tired. He was on Rolling H property—and he might catch sight of Lisa Holcroft again.

The memory of her dark-haired, blue-eyed beauty

sent his heart racing until he thought it might leap from his chest.

"You're lookin' mighty happy for a man who's missing a meal and not going to get much sleep for another day," Texas observed. "Is there something I don't know?"

"Any chance we might see Miss Holcroft?"

"So that's it? You got your cap set for that filly?" Texas shook his head. "Don't bother. Her daddy's foreman's got her in his corral already. Fact is, Whitey might end up owning the Rolling H 'fore sundown."

"How's that?"

Texas blinked. "You are a curious mix of bright and pure dumb, John Allen. Who do you think that gent is ridin' in the back of the wagon?"

"I saw him talking to Mr. Kincaid in Chugwater the other day when we went in to get the bags of coal for the smithy. Another rancher," John said. He frowned as he worked over Texas' words. Then details fell into place like an avalanche. In the light of noonday Wyoming he saw the distinctive features of the man's face and recognized Lisa Holcroft's father.

"Yep," Texas said. "That's Charles Holcroft, owner of more land than you can ride across in a week. And if you started eating a prime Delmonico steak right now and kept eating fast as you could, you'd never come close to finishing off his herd 'fore you died of a burst gut."

John had nothing to say. He stared at the wounded man, a silent prayer intended to add to Holcroft's innate toughness. He had not realized who the rustlers' victim had been.

"There's the house." Texas took off his hat and waved to get their attention. Several men came from the bunkhouse, one running to the ranch house.

With them came the trim figure John immediately recognized as Lisa Holcroft.

He didn't have to be told the man standing next to her was the Rolling H foreman, Whitey Yarbrough. A streak of snow white ran through the center of his black hair. John thought it made the man look like a skunk, but he held his tongue as Texas reined in by the ranch house porch.

"We got Mr. Holcroft in the back," the cook called. "You folks best fetch a doctor to look at him. He's in a bad way."

John jumped from the wagon, intending to help the Rolling H hands get Holcroft from the rear. He wasn't needed. They crowded close and pushed him back, as if touching their boss might somehow end his life rather than help save it. John drifted over to the porch and looked up at Lisa Holcroft. The woman chewed her lower lip and stood on tiptoe in an attempt to catch sight of her father.

"Rustlers, Miss Holcroft," John said. "Rustlers did this. They tried to steal a few head from our herd and then they raced off. Your pa got between them and safety." John saw how she frowned.

"Mind if I ask a question, ma'am? What was your pa doing out riding alone at night?"

Whitey Yarbrough came over, pushing between John and Lisa Holcroft.

"You got no call asking her questions," the foreman said. "This isn't the time or place. You brought her pa in. For that we thank you, but you got no call asking any questions right now."

"Sorry," John said, his hackles rising. Yarbrough was polite enough, if a bit brusque, but he didn't cotton to the way he put his arm around Lisa's waist and drew her close. It wasn't right to show such affection in front of others. She didn't take notice because of her worry for her father.

"We've been having trouble with rustlers, too," Yarbrough went on, moving Lisa so she was out of the way as the wranglers carried her father into the ranch house. The foreman bent over and whispered something in the woman's ear. She nodded and started after her father.

Lisa paused, turned and gave John a wan smile. She said, "I don't mean to be rude. Thank you for what you've done. It is appreciated. Truly, it is." And then she vanished into the house.

John went to touch the brim of his hat but the woman was gone too quick to receive even this little gesture of respect from him. John knew he looked a fright to the lovely woman, his clothes dirty from the roundup and chasing rustlers and a two-day stubble of beard turning his chin into a prickly pear cactus. He wished he could have made a better impression, though he knew being the best dressed dude in all of Wyoming wouldn't have gotten him noticed much more because of her pa's sorry condition.

"As I was saying, the rustlers been working our range too. Mr. Holcroft must have ridden out last night to do some tracking. In his day, there was none better."

"He seemed to be doing a good job of it when they came across him," John said, defending Holcroft's abilities as a scout, though he knew nothing about the man save that he had a lovely daughter. "They didn't give him any chance to defend himself. They rode by and gunned him down."

Yarbrough shook his head. "They're mean ones, that's a fact. Now why don't you and your partner get on back to the Flying K? We both got jobs to do."

Yarbrough spun and went into the house, never giving John so much as another glance.

"Reckon I know when we been dismissed like a pair of misbehavin' kids," Texas said. "You'd think they'd at least offer us a sip of water to cut the dust in our throat." The cook snorted and climbed back into the wagon, waiting impatiently for John to follow.

John climbed in, his head craned around as they drove off. He hoped for another glimpse of Lisa but she stayed inside the house. John spent the rest of the trip glum and withdrawn, lost in a world of his own black thoughts.

Chapter Nine

"Sorry to hear about Holcroft," Warner Kincaid said, shaking his head. "The rustlers have to be stopped before they kill someone."

"Any word on how Mr. Holcroft's doing?" John asked. "He looked mighty pale when Texas and I got him over to the Rolling H."

"I'll ride on over and inquire after his health when we're finished with the day's work," Kincaid said. "Bill tells me you're doing a fine job with the ironmongering— and you're not half bad when it comes to riding herd on the beeves."

John smiled crookedly. The roundup had been underway for two days now and he still found it hard staying in the saddle longer than an hour at a time. His rear end felt like a piece of ground meat and every bone in his body hurt from the constant jolting gait of Old Sadie. And she was one of the easiest horses to ride in the Flying K corral. He had thought smithing to be taxing work. John never realized how much more difficult it was being a cowboy.

And he loved every second of it.

"I do what I can."

"You're a fine addition to the Flying K outfit," Kincaid said, gracing him with one of his all too infrequent smiles. "Where are Bill and the others working right now?"

John scratched his head. He had ridden night herd for Cassidy and was asleep when the wranglers rode out in the morning. Without a spare horse, it didn't take long to wear out Old Sadie—and in a way, John was glad for that. As much thrill as he got out of working the cattle, he needed more sleep than he was getting.

"Don't know, but I think they're moving toward yon bluff."

"Painted Rock? Haven't seen many cows in that direction for a year or three," Kincaid allowed. "Still, if the herd's thin in this pasture, Bill might be right thinking they had moved higher to get juicier grass. Ride with me, John, and tell me all about finding Charles Holcroft."

John's belly rumbled from lack of food and his body refused to move right from too many kinks earned riding most of the night, but he couldn't turn down this request from his boss.

"Be glad to, sir," he said, grabbing his saddle and

walking to Old Sadie. The mare turned a disapproving eye on him but she let him throw the blanket and saddle on with no fuss. Her days of protesting even this mistreatment were long past. In a way, John was happy to have such an even-tempered mount, though riding Arroyo would bring him some notoriety with the other cowpunchers.

He and Kincaid rode side by side, John noting from the corner of his eye how tired the man appeared. His face was thinner than before and the pallor gave him a half-dead mien. If possible, he looked worse riding in the saddle than Holcroft had sprawled on the ground with a bullet in his chest.

"You and Mr. Holcroft close friends?" John asked.

"Not really. We've been neighbors for years." Kincaid fell silent for a moment, lost in distant memories. "Reckon we were closer when both our wives were living. Ruth died about the same time Charlie's wife did. Diphtheria, it was. Killed half the people in Wyoming, or so it seemed at the time. The ladies kept us together with socials and barn dances and even occasional picnics on Sundays after church. We've drifted apart, Charlie and I, not seeing much of one another save for the chance meetings in Chugwater or at the cattle growers' meetings."

John licked his lips, wondering if he ought to speak on another subject close to his heart. Before he realized he was doing so, he blurted out, "What about Miss Holcroft?"

"Lisa? A good girl. She's the spitting image of her ma. Lovely lady, simply lovely."

John knew it was out of line pursuing this. Instead he asked, "Do you have any children? Never heard mention of any."

"They died. No, not of diphtheria. Four of them Ruth and I saw to the grave. Accidents and sickness cut through them all like a scythe and only Aaron lived to see his thirteenth birthday. The day after, in fact, he was caught in a landslide over near Painted Rock, where we're heading." He let out a deep, shuddery sigh and looked even older and more tired than before. "The Flying K is the only kin I have now."

John started to apologize, realizing how he opened old sores. Before he could say anything, Kincaid rose in his stirrups and put his hand to his forehead to shield his eyes from the sun's glare.

"What is it?" John asked.

"Can't say for certain. A powerful lot of men are gathered about where Bill's supposed to be working."

John saw what his boss had already seen when they rode a few hundred yards closer. Topping a rise, they looked down on a grassy area holding more than two hundred head of cattle. The Flying K wranglers were busy with branding iron and rope—and the other cowboys sat astride their horses in a half circle around them. John didn't have to be told that trouble was brewing.

Not a one of the mounted cowboys simply held the

reins in their hands. All had either rifle or six-shooter close to hand.

"Those are Rolling H men," Kincaid said. "Let's see what the fuss is all about." He put his spurs to his horse's flanks and shot off. John followed at a more leisurely trot, not able to make Old Sadie go any faster. By the time he arrived, all the cowboys were on the ground and squared off.

He recognized the Rolling H foreman, Whitey Yarbrough, instantly. The shock of white hair nestled along the top of his scalp shone like a beacon in the bright sunlight.

"Those are our beeves. All the cattle have Rolling H brands. The calves are ours." Yarbrough shoved out his chin in a belligerent way, daring Bill to make something of it. The Rolling H cowboys outnumbered Kincaid's men two to one. Even if they had not, the firepower resting on their hips and in saddle sheaths formed a danger to be reckoned with.

John kicked out of the saddle and went to stand beside Kincaid.

"Whitey," the older man started, "these disputes happen all the time. I'm sure Bill has good reason to think the mavericks are ours."

"Don't want to be disrespectful, Mr. Kincaid," Yarbrough said, obviously intending just that, "but you're stealin' our calves." His brother Sam moved up beside him, hand on the sweat-stained oak handle of his six-shooter. John saw how keyed up Sam Yarbrough was. The slightest provocation would set him off and lead would fly.

"A maverick is a maverick. Some of those cows might be carrying a Rolling H on their hips," Kincaid allowed, "but some don't. See that heifer over yonder? The one with the ear missing?"

"What of it?" Yarbrough put his hands on his hips, as if ready to fight.

"I remember it losing that ear when it was just a calf nursing at its mama's udder. It got caught on a strand of barbed wire out back of my corral. You wouldn't believe the fuss it made until I got it free, but there was no saving its ear."

"That's Rolling H stock," Yarbrough said, his tone increasingly belligerent.

"Seems as if there's only one way to settle this," Bill said, stepping forward. His hand rested on the six–gun at his side. John caught his breath. Before he could say a word to head off the fight that might turn deadly, a cheer went up from both sides.

"A fight! That'll settle it!"

John glanced at Kincaid. His boss had a pained expression but didn't seem too perturbed at the notion of men shooting it out over a cow.

"Who'll it be, Whitey?" Bill asked.

"My brother's 'bout the best we have. Go on, Sam. You show 'em who's top dog on this range."

Sam Yarbrough stepped forward, rolling up his

sleeves to show muscular arms corded with veins like steel cabling. John stared openmouthed. They weren't going to gun down one another. Rather, they were settling the dispute with fisticuffs.

"Lou, get on over here," Bill called. "Lou Cassidy's our man. He'll show you what's what."

The two squared off, fists clenched and circling warily as they each waited for the other to make the first move.

"Boredom," muttered Kincaid, more to himself than to John. "There's no call for this, save that it breaks up the tedium of a roundup."

"The winner gets the calf?"

"That's the way it works." For all his disgust at the fight, Kincaid made no move to stop it.

John felt his pulse pounding faster. He stepped forward. He knew something about pugilism, having been the best fighter in the Nebraska mines. But both these men danced around more than they fought. He found himself studying Sam Yarbrough, hunting for new weaknesses he might exploit if they ever fought.

A flurry of blows rocked back Cassidy, then he responded in kind, getting in a powerful left to Yarbrough's belly. John remembered hitting Yarbrough there and feeling as if he had rammed his fist into a brick wall. Lou rapidly found that he needed more strength in his punches to stop Yarbrough with body blows.

"The chin, Lou!" John called. "Go for the chin. He's got a glass jaw!"

John's suggestion was lost amid the jeers and catcalls

from the gathered cowboys. Some bet on the outcome and others simply watched, but the din was deafening. The boredom of their hard work momentarily forgotten, the men vented their steam cheering on their champion and disparaging his opponent.

John saw Lou beginning to slow, to weaken, to let in blows that further sapped his strength. The few blows he got in were glancing or weak and did no damage. Somehow, Yarbrough fed on the minor abuse he withstood at Lou's hands. A quick punch to Lou's belly almost doubled him over. Yarbrough finished with an uppercut that staggered Lou, sending him stumbling backward into the crowd. Two Flying K wranglers caught him and kept him from falling insensate to the ground.

"That's it," Bill called, seeing Lou's eyes glaze over from the punch. "Yarbrough wins. That's the Rolling H's calf."

"No, no!" shouted Yarbrough, spinning around. He wiped his bloodied knuckles on his shirt and then pointed straight at John. "I want to fight him now."

A new round of cheers wasn't needed for John to step forward. He was game, but not to fight Yarbrough. His eyes locked with Whitey Yarbrough's.

"I've beaten him once," John said loud enough for all to hear. "I'll challenge the Rolling H foreman. You man enough to face me, Whitey?" John wasn't sure why he issued the challenge, but he realized it had to do with taking the man's measure. If Whitey Yarbrough was going to marry Lisa Holcroft, he had better be one accomplished man to be worthy of her.

"No, I want to fight him. He sucker punched me. He—"

"Hush up, Sam," Whitey Yarbrough snapped at his brother. The foreman stepped up and let his eyes run up and down John, as if trying to figure him out. "You're the wrangler who fetched Mr. Holcroft back the other day, aren't you?"

"And you're the one going to step into the circle with me." John drew a large circle with the toe of his boot, marking a crude ring. "The first to cry uncle or step outside the ring loses."

New roars of approval rose, a few catcalls mixed in with them. The men wanted only the spectacle of a fight and didn't care about the reason for it. Truth was, John wasn't too sure why he was doing this. He knew he could beat Whitey's brother—he had already done so back on the train. But why fight the Rolling H foreman?

John found himself thinking about what Lisa would say when it got back to her that he had knocked out her fiancé. If it were a fair fight, would that matter to her? John wasn't sure of himself or his motives any more. If he wanted to impress the woman, knocking off Yarbrough's head wasn't the way to do it.

And yet, and yet . . .

He wanted to see what kind of a man had won the lovely woman's heart.

He stepped inside the ring and lifted his doubled fists. Whitey stared at him, then backed away a half step.

"There's no need for a fight. Wouldn't prove anything. And we got work to do. Sam, get those mavericks cut from the herd. The rest of you! Why are you standing around? Get mounted. We've got a roundup to finish."

Yarbrough shot a hot look at John, then spun and stalked off. John stood watching him, feeling stupid with his fists still clenched and raised. He lowered them and knew the white stripe running through Yarbrough's hair went down his back—and in a different color.

Chapter Ten

The fire wasn't hot enough. He didn't have a proper anvil. The scrap iron he used to fix the branding iron refused to fall into place. John Allen found a thousand reasons for being irritable and not doing as good a job as he usually did when he worked metal. He shoved the cracked branding iron into the fire as if too much speed would make it hotter.

"John, why don't you follow Lou up the canyon and see if you can't find a few of those strays? The other wranglers are scattered to the four winds to the south and we need someone riding in the other direction." Bill Diamond stared down at him from his vantage in the smithy doorway, aware something was eating at his insides.

"Got to finish fixing this iron," John said. He pulled it from the fire and halfheartedly banged at it with his

107

hammer. It refused to shape the way he wanted so he hammered even harder and got an even worse result.

"Losing a few head doesn't matter that much, even if it was to Whitey Yarbrough."

This caused John to look up, more heat in his eyes than in his forge.

"You and him friends? You worked together pretty well. And I saw you two shaking hands before he rode out with our mavericks."

"I was trying to mend fences. Wyoming's a big place, but not that big when you bump up against bad attitudes. We've got to work together out here. It might be days or weeks between seeing another human on the range. When you do, it helps if you are peaceable."

John tried to put his feelings into words. Yarbrough had backed down when called out to a fair fight. The man was a coward, no matter what excuse he used. Yet no one else in either outfit had seen the fight or the evasion the way John had. They had been disappointed at the lack of excitement afforded them but hadn't thought Whitey was a yellow-belly.

"I'm always a friendly sort," John said, "but not when they take our cattle like that. What do they need with a few extra calves, anyway? The Rolling H has thousands of head and we're scraping by with scrawny mavericks. And even those are fair game for the rustlers."

"Every one matters," Bill admitted, pushing back his floppy brimmed white hat and wiping sweat from his forehead. "We don't like losing even one. No reason

Whitey would, either. That's why he's foreman of the biggest spread in these parts. He looks after Mr. Holcroft's interests, no matter what."

John finished banging on the iron. It was a sloppy job but would hold for a few more brandings. He held the branding iron up and critically studied it. "Not my best work," he said finally, "but it will serve you 'til I get back. What direction did Lou head?"

"Don't worry much about finding him. Just take on out and get the stragglers moving back in this direction for him to brand later."

"You want me on day herd?" John rose and shook the dust from his clothing. "Looks as if I'm moving up in the world."

"You're a hard worker, John, that I will give you," the foreman said. "I don't understand why you want to move cattle when you can be hammering away at your iron. This is a real profession. Wrangling cattle is nothing but tedious, backbreaking work with no real future. Look at me, all broke down and wanting to do anything else."

"Can you tell me why you're here instead of San Francisco or New Orleans or Boston?"

"Cattle's the only life I know. It's a hard one and I wish I knew another trade, but I don't." Bill stared at John curiously, then shook his head. "Being shorthanded and all, I want you pulling leather during the daylight too. Can you do that and still mend the ironwork as it breaks?"

"Do two men's jobs? I'm up to it," John said, smiling.

He had finally broken into the ranks of the wranglers, accepted by the foreman as a cowpuncher. A greenhorn cowpuncher, to be sure, but one nonetheless to be trusted on his own. He gathered his gear and saddled Old Sadie, wishing he had Arroyo under him. The mare never complained but she never moved too fast, either. Her one speed was all he was likely to get, no matter what demands he placed on her. Somehow, he didn't have the heart to put on spurs and use them on her scrawny flanks.

As he rode out, John glanced back over his shoulder at the main house. Kincaid spoke with his foreman, and Bill was shaking his head. John knew the roundup wasn't going well for the Flying K outfit. Calves were few and far between this season. Bill might gainsay it but losing even one to the Rolling H hurt bad. A single calf gone equalled the foreman's pay for the summer. Unless Mr. Kincaid got his loan from the reluctant banker, Charles Holcroft's offer to buy the ranch might be the only course open to him.

John knew such a loss might kill Kincaid. He had more than a simple livelihood tied up in the Flying K. He had memories.

Other thoughts intruded. Holcroft might not be in any condition to pursue the offer, depending on the severity of the wound he took. The rustlers might have sealed a man's death—and the loss of the Flying K to bank creditors. It didn't seem fair. A single bullet might spell doom on two spreads in different ways.

An hour's ride took John to a branch in the faint trail he followed. Not much good as a tracker, he thought Cassidy and the two others with him had ridden into the canyon, but plaintive lowing drew him away from that path. He sucked in a lungful of air and Old Sadie did too. The way the mare surged with newfound energy told him his own nose hadn't lied.

"Water ahead, Sadie. Let's drink our fill. And maybe find a few mavericks doing likewise." John heard hooves clicking on stone and more lowing. Definitely cattle ahead, though who they might belong to was something he would have to discover.

In a way, he hoped he would run across Whitey Yarbrough again. He felt he had a score to settle with the Rolling H foreman. And then again, John wasn't sure what the score was. Marrying a woman as fine as Lisa Holcroft was no crime. Quite the contrary. It was a coup. With Charles Holcroft so badly injured, a quick marriage might put the Rolling H's deed in Yarbrough's hip pocket.

"Whoa," John called, tugging on the reins. Old Sadie reluctantly stopped. A pond of fresh, sparkling water gleamed like a diamond in the afternoon sun. And drinking at it were a score of cattle, ranging from calves to feisty old breeding cows.

"We'll check the calves to see if they're carrying brands, then find their mamas," John said, talking to Old Sadie as if she cared. The horse's nostrils flared as she strained to reach the water. John dismounted and led the horse forward, reluctant to let her have her fill. He had seen horses bloat in a few minutes, not knowing when to stop drinking.

As thirsty as he was, John knew Old Sadie wouldn't bloat until he got back. He walked to the nearest cow and found the rear end all covered in mud. The cow protested him wiping away the cloaking mud. His heart sank when he saw a brand he didn't recognize burned into the hide. He traced out the pattern with his forefinger as he tried to make sense of it.

"Square Seven," he mused. "Never heard of that outfit. Must have walked a ways to end up smack dab between Rolling H and Flying K herds." He worked around to the calves eyeing them carefully, disappointed when he discovered the same brand. He went to a heifer that tried to bolt as he approached and noted the Square 7 brand—but this time he paused as he examined the burn.

Something didn't set right. It took him a couple of minutes to figure what it was. As he worked on it, he went to pull Old Sadie from the stock pond. He led the horse to a grassy area and tied the reins to a low-growing blackberry bush. The horse nickered and contentedly began cropping the grass in a tasty meal.

"That's not the right brand," John said aloud, as an idea formed. He wasn't experienced enough to know for certain, but he thought the brand on that yearling cow looked mighty ragged. Retracing his footsteps he found the aggrieved heifer again.

He frowned as he deliberately traced out the pattern

burned in the hairy side. At first glance, the Square 7 looked prominent but he saw how another brand might have been laid on the cow under this one—a Rolling H brand.

He walked a ways from the pond and caught two more cows. The Square 7 brand was off by fractions of an inch—and the brand beneath it clearly showed.

"Flying K," he said, anger mounting. "Somebody's taking Flying K and Rolling H cattle and putting their own brand on them. That's outright stealing!"

John stomped back to the muddy bank and examined every hindquarter he could find. Only two cattle carried a brand other than the Square 7—and the two Rolling H cows shied when he approached, skittish as if they suspected he might try to run their brand. John knew this was only his imagination hard at work when he put such motives into a cow's head, but he couldn't deny what was going on at their flanks.

There was more than one way to steal a cow. Riding in and driving out a few head from a big herd was outright rustling. Finding a cow on the range and changing its brand to a spurious one was no less thieving than using a gun to stick up a bank.

He considered what to do and figured the best way of dealing with this was to drive a few head of the brand altered cattle back to the Flying K camp. With firsthand evidence of rustlers running a brand, maybe Kincaid could go to the Wyoming Stock Growers Association and find who had been selling Square 7-branded cattle. The man claiming ownership of those cows would be responsible for stealing thousands—tens of thousands!—of dollars worth of beef on the hoof.

John yanked the reins from the bush and moved around Old Sadie to put his boot in the dangling stirrup. He froze when he heard steps behind him. The distinctive metallic sound of a six-shooter cocking echoed like thunder in his ears.

"Don't make a move," came a cold voice, "or I'll put a slug in your head."

Chapter Eleven

"Turn around real slow," came the command. "I've got the drop on you, so don't try anything, you varmint."

John Allen held his hands out where his unseen attacker could see them. He did as he was told. When he saw the man behind the six-shooter, his jaw dropped.

"Carver!"

"Well, well, imagine finding you out here pokin' around my cows," Carver Norton said. The man let down the hammer of his six-gun and tucked the pistol back into its soft leather holster slung low on his hip. "Should have figured our trails would cross one day. Didn't think it would be so soon or out by a watering hole."

"How are you, Carver?" John thrust out his hand. Carver shook it hard.

"Doing fine. Seems that you are too. Those are different calluses on your hand from the last time we shook. You workin' the herd now?"

"I am," John said, motioning back in the direction of the pond. "Let's find some shade and talk. It's too hot in the afternoon to stand around and get sunstroke."

"I got time to palaver. That's about all I do these days that amounts to anything. The herd's thin this year, mighty sparse grazing all winter. I swear, if this weather goes on like this much longer, there won't be a cow worth mentioning anywhere in Wyoming."

"I know," John said, lamenting with his friend over the few calves the Flying K wranglers were finding. "I was ready to go find my foreman."

"Why bother? None of these are yours," Carver said, his arm encompassing all the cattle at the pond.

"Have you looked at the brands?"

"Not real close. I ride on by if I don't see a Rolling H—or an unbranded hindquarter. What's so all-fired interesting that you'd ride back to tell ol' Bill Diamond about it? These aren't yours. Or mine."

John grabbed the tail of one cow and pulled it around so the two could study the brand carefully. Carver let out a low whistle and pushed his hat back.

"If that don't take all," he said. "There's more rustling going on in these parts than I thought. And damn me for not paying more attention to other brands."

"Most all these carry a Square Seven brand. Where's that spread?"

"Never heard of it, but over a cold winter and on the open range, a cow might wander a hundred miles or more. Some stay close to the ranch house to get stored hay, others are more adventurous and go looking for fodder." Carver checked a few other brands, then went to sit with his back against a willow trunk. He pulled out fixings and worked to build himself a cigarette. He started to offer the tobacco to John, then stopped.

"You haven't picked up any vices since Cheyenne City, have you? Didn't think so." Carver put the tobacco pouch back into his shirt pocket and took out a friction match. It hissed as he scraped it along the tree trunk. Seconds later, he was inhaling deeply. Smoke curled up around his face and momentarily hid it as he considered what John had showed him.

"What are we going to do about the fake brands?" John thought frontier justice was more likely to prevail than letting the authorities deal with the crime. The sheriff wasn't as inclined to spend time tracking down the rustlers running a brand as were the men having their stock stolen.

"What do you think? I have to get on back and let Whitey know. You were on the track to doin' the right thing if you were going to tell Bill." Carver inhaled again, closed his eyes and leaned back.

John stared at his friend, noting how tired Carver looked.

"Been a long, hard roundup," Carver said when he noticed John's attention. "I can't remember the number of times I've ridden night herd, only to go out hunting strays during the day."

"The Rolling H has a lot of wranglers. Why the double duty?"

"You're standin' double duty, too, aren't you? You've got the drawn look. Leastways, you look like I feel. But to answer that question. The Flying K is running a dozen cowpunchers short."

"But not the Rolling H," John pressed. "We ran into Yarbrough and his brother and some others. They had enough men to let you get some sleep."

"Can't rightly say where most of the men go," Carver said. "Always more'n a few hands short." He chuckled and looked at John. "I heard about the fight between Sam Yarbrough and Lou Cassidy."

"What about me challenging Whitey Yarbrough?" John felt his ire rising again.

"One of the boys mentioned it in passing. I thought it might have been you. Nobody else is crazy enough to egg on a man like Whitey. He's a steady enough rider unless you push him too far. Then he and his brother act a lot more alike than usual."

"They're both hotheads," John said. He took a deep breath, then changed the subject. "How's Mr. Holcroft getting on?"

"Weak, but he'll recover just fine. The doc took the bullet out where it lodged against a rib. And," Carver said, the twinkle coming into his eyes, "he's got a real good nurse."

"Lisa? Miss Holcroft?" John sat up straighter.

"Of course. Who else might it be?" Carver enjoyed teasing John.

"Don't rightly know. A man with Mr. Holcroft's wealth could hire anyone."

"But none so pretty and caring. Heard tell that she's a fine cook too."

John knew Carver poked him just to watch him squirm.

"She's spoken for. Can't see what she finds interesting in a man like Whitey Yarbrough."

"You don't know him too well. And don't go judgin' him by his brother. Sam's a strange one, always riding off in the night and all."

"How's that?"

Carver shrugged. "Shouldn't speak out of turn like that. It just seems that Sam's gone more than he's in camp. I was riding night herd a few days back and I saw Sam slinkin' into camp just before sunup. His brother covers for him, but a few of the other wranglers are starting to gossip." Carver snorted and got to his feet. "Sometimes, it gets so lonely out here men sound like old women at a quilting bee, thinking up things to prattle about."

"You think he might be rustling?"

"Never said that," Carver said sharply. A sly smile curled his lips as he relaxed back against the tree trunk. "Can't help thinking it, though. I'd better find Whitey and let him know about the Square Seven laid over our branded cattle. You do the same with Bill Diamond. He's a good man."

"Good seeing you again," John said, brushing himself off. "I hope our trails will cross again soon."

"You know they will—if you're going to the hoedown."

"What hoedown?"

"The one Miss Holcroft's going to attend," Carver said. He touched the brim of his Stetson in mock salute and rode off before John could question him further.

"What hoedown?" he shouted after the departing cowboy. All he got in way of answer was laughter.

He took off his hat and threw it at the ground in frustration. Carver took too much delight in tormenting him. What hoedown? Lisa was going? When?

John picked up his hat and returned to Old Sadie. He climbed into the saddle, counted the cattle carrying the Square 7 brand, and then started back to the Flying K camp. But after he had ridden, deep in thought, for almost an hour John realized he had veered off course. He reined back and looked around.

"Where're those cliffs Lou and the others rode toward?" He tried to locate them and couldn't. John realized he had not been paying attention as he rode and had gotten lost like a greenhorn. He tilted his head back and studied the sun to afford him some clues. It dipped low in the west, giving him his bearings. He had ridden a tad south of the real trail back to camp and had gone miles out of his way. He urged Old Sadie back in the proper direction.

"I won't be thinking on Lisa Holcroft or any hoedown this time," he assured his horse. The mare turned her head, shot him a look of complete disbelief at such an improbability, then put her head down and started walking stolidly in the right direction.

John had to laugh. The horse knew him better than most of the men on the roundup. He rode along at the mare's pace, growing restive when he realized the sun was sinking faster than it ought to due to the high mountains cutting off the bright afternoon light.

"We need to get back to camp before sundown or Bill will have the whole outfit out looking for us," he said. John didn't cotton much to the idea that the foreman would think him so much a greenhorn that he had to be treated differently from the others.

"That way. We can cut close to the cliff and angle into the camp in jig time," John decided. It would cut almost a half hour off the ride now that he knew the country and where he headed.

He hadn't ridden fifteen minutes when he heard the heavy thudding of hoofbeats. A rider came fast and furious along a trail parallel to the one he rode. John stood in the stirrups and stared into the twilight to find the rider. He was close enough to the Flying K camp that the rider might be one of his trailmates.

"Sam Yarbrough," he said under his breath, recognizing

the Rolling H foreman's brother. John settled down and frowned. Where did Yarbrough ride hellbent for leather at this time of day? He remembered Carver's remarks about Yarbrough taking off at night and not returning until early morning—the time a rustler might be gone from his bunkhouse.

Rustlers.

The word burned in John's brain like a heated branding iron. Finding the Square 7 cattle with their altered brands might be important, but getting solid evidence against one of the rustlers seemed a better reason for returning to camp.

"Come on, Sadie," John urged, putting his heels into the tired horse's flanks. "We've got ourselves a rustler to hogtie." Thoughts of catching Yarbrough in the act of stealing cattle fired his imagination. No thought of reward entered his head. John was more inclined to risk getting shot like Charles Holcroft simply to bring the outlaws to justice.

He got the horse onto the trail behind the hard-riding Yarbrough. No matter how much he tried, John couldn't get any more speed out of Old Sadie. The mare had a mind of her own and ignored his need to hurry.

John finally sank into the saddle, contenting himself with the deliberate pace the horse set. Now and then John rose to try to keep Yarbrough in view. There was no reason for the man to be riding so hard and fast near the Flying K camp unless he was up to no good.

The thought drifted across John's mind that Yarbrough

might be going to speak with Bill or Kincaid, but then he saw a branch in the trail and evidence Yarbrough had ridden that way. He rode elsewhere—and what business did he have?

By now the sun had set and twilight passed gently into deeper night. Old Sadie never flagged but she did not speed up, either. For this surefooted pursuit of Yarbrough, John was thankful. The horse wasn't going to break a leg any more than she was likely to come up on the rustler unexpectedly.

"He's up to no good," John said. "What might he be doing near the Flying K herd? Hunting for strays? Or running a brand?"

Old Sadie whinnied and shook him out of his reverie. He had no proof Yarbrough was up to anything illegal. That was why he followed him, to get the evidence. This was Wyoming Territory and part of the United States. John was a firm believer that a man was innocent until proven guilty. No matter how little he liked Yarbrough, the man hadn't been hauled into court yet.

"I'll find evidence that will convince any jury," he said to himself.

Old Sadie whinnied again. This time John heeded the warning and reined back. He led the mare from the trail and tethered her near a thick clump of grass. Advancing on foot, he stumbled on rocks and almost twisted his ankle. He finally flopped belly down atop a rock and peered over it.

Voices drifted on the wind—two voices.

Ahead he saw Yarbrough bathed in a shaft of silvery moonlight. The man with him stood in shadow, no more than a dim silhouette. Yarbrough and the mysterious man argued for several minutes. Try as he might, John couldn't make heads or tails of their conversation.

They might be talking about rustling every cow in Wyoming or they might be discussing how bad the winter had been. He simply could not tell.

But why was Yarbrough meeting a man after dark in this fashion?

John decided to sneak closer. He was no trailsman but he might get near enough to the pair to eavesdrop and learn their business. It might be honest, or it might concern rustling. He had to find out.

As John slid down the side of the rock like a lizard, Yarbrough let out a snort of pure disgust, swung in the saddle and rode away as hard as he had come to the rendezvous. In only seconds he was gone, swallowed by the darkness.

John kept moving as quietly as possible and came out near the spot where the two men had talked. Of the shadowy figure he found no trace. He hadn't heard a horse ride off nor did he see any footpath for the man to take. The hidden man had vanished as if he had been nothing more than a ghost.

John went back to where Old Sadie contentedly cropped grass. The horse started as he neared, then settled down when she recognized him. She didn't even protest too much when he climbed into the saddle. Old

Sadie was as eager to get out of here as John. He had quite a story to tell. Or did he?

"Back to camp," he said to the horse. The more he thought on it, the less sure he was he had discovered any-thing worth relating to Bill or Kincaid. He felt only dis-gust with himself that he had been so ineffective finding out Yarbrough's clandestine business. "I don't know what I'm going to tell Bill, but there's not much I can say about Sam Yarbrough that won't get me laughed at. Bill and Sam's brother are tight. Better to worry about the Square Seven cattle first, I reckon. That I can prove."

But he still fretted over the secret meeting. Who rode out to talk with Yarbrough? And what had they dis-cussed so angrily?

Chapter Twelve

John Allen wasn't satisfied with the foreman telling him to keep the discovery of the Square 7 cattle under his hat. For a week John had worked and stewed and grown increasingly unsure that Bill's advice was all that good. He had ridden back to camp after spying on Sam Yarbrough, not sure what to report.

The rustlers running the Rolling H brand—and probably the Flying K's as well—hadn't surprised Bill Diamond the way John thought it might. If anything, it seemed only to be another piece of evidence for the foreman to add to his already great store about the widespread rustling. But nothing had been done, and this galled John something fierce.

The intervening week had been filled with long

nights and longer days for John. He worked in the smithy to keep the branding irons in good repair, not that they were needed much. Occasional stints at night herd lengthened into even longer days hunting for mavericks. The wranglers found a few hundred calves wandering the prairie without brands—and no more. For a harsh winter, this might be a decent enough herd to move back toward the Flying K ranch house, but Kincaid needed more to keep the ranch solvent. By John's inexpert but carefully considered reckoning, the less than thousand cattle, new calves, heifers and older cows, would barely cover operating expenses.

"What are you doing?" Texas asked, peering over John's shoulder at the foolscap filled with his calculations. "I didn't know you could cipher."

"I'm trying to figure how many head Mr. Kincaid needs to keep the Flying K running."

"You can do that?" The grizzled old cook scratched his week-long growth of bristly beard. "Mr. Kincaid don't do much of that hisself, leastways not since the missus died. He kinda goes along, spending what he needs and not doing too much planning."

"That might be part of the Flying K's trouble," John said. "I'm not saying anything against Mr. Kincaid or Bill, but they could spend less and get more if they changed the way they do things."

"Don't tell me any of it," the cook said, clapping hands over his ears and shaking his head. "Gives me a headache thinkin' on matters like that. Every time anyone talks about money, it always means I got to order fewer beans and find more weeds growin' 'round here to stretch what I do fix. Next thing I know, they'll have me goin' out to the cattle's salt lick if I want any spicing up for my meals."

"Salt? What a good idea," John said. "Never tasted any in your cooking, but then it's hard to taste anything but the loco weed you put in to give it body."

"I don't see you complainin' none when it comes to eating my chow, John Allen."

John folded the sheet of paper where he had been doing his calculations. Admittedly, he was making a lot of wild guesses about the Flying K's budget and what all was spent keeping the ranch going, but he didn't think he was too far off. He had kept the books for the gunsmith he had apprenticed to and had gotten a feel for expenses. No business could be improved, John had been told, without a good set of accounting books showing where money went and how it came in.

From what John could tell, Kincaid's trouble was as much poor control of what he spent as it was lack of beeves to move to a railhead.

"We got to keep working," Texas said. "We'll be back at the ranch before you know it and then, and then!"

"Then what?" John asked.

"The hoedown. We got to mind our Ps and Qs so Mr. Kincaid will let us go into Chugwater for the hoedown."

John's heart jumped in his chest. He had forgotten about the hoedown Carver Norton had mentioned.

"It'll be a chance to let off some steam before getting back onto the range."

"Who all goes to this hoedown?" John tried to keep his voice level.

"Everybody from a hundred miles off. It's about the biggest social event in Chugwater. The first month of roundup is usually the hardest, since we spend so much time on the range. Fattening the cattle and tending them on the way to Cheyenne comes after the hoedown."

"Everybody goes?" John repeated.

"Even the folks from the Rolling H," Texas said. He had a look that reminded John of Carver Norton. "Heard tell even Miss Holcroft will be there, but that wouldn't concern you any, would it?"

"Not at all." John felt himself flushing and turned away to keep the cook from noticing. Texas laughed heartily, warning John that his reaction would soon be common knowledge throughout the camp. But he could tolerate any joshing for the chance to see Lisa again.

"Gather round, men!" Kincaid called. The Flying K's owner climbed onto a lightning-struck stump and waited for his wranglers to make their way to him. "I want to thank you for the hard work you've put in."

"Little enough resulted from it," grumbled one man. John shot the man, Henry Jackson, a dark look. Jackson had done nothing but complain since they had begun the roundup. Seeing the attention John paid, Jackson said defiantly, "If we worked for a good outfit, we'd have ten times the calves in the herd." He fell silent when Kincaid continued.

"You've worked hard for little money. Since we've rounded up all our herd and added a few mavericks to it, there's only one thing left to do."

Kincaid paused and let the cowpunchers come to their own conclusions. Then he said brightly, "We'll get back to the ranch and then you can go to the Chugwater hoedown!"

A wild cheer rose. Too many had expected Kincaid to say they had to stay and repair bridles or minister to the sick cattle. Too many this year carried some wasting disease. No buying agent for an Eastern slaughterhouse would purchase an obviously ill cow. The offending beeves had to be treated and brought back to health during the drive to Cheyenne City to turn the highest profit possible.

"The hoedown's this weekend, Saturday night starting at sundown. I want you all to act like gentleman and I don't want to have to bail out a single one of you from the town jail."

"He might not have the money," Jackson said under his breath. Seeing John's hot glare of disapproval, the wrangler muttered to himself and walked off.

John turned back to Kincaid. The Flying K owner continued to praise his men, even promising bonuses if they delivered the herd to the Cheyenne railhead before the Rolling H herd arrived. But John listened less to the man's words than he did to the messages Kincaid's body sent. The man's hands shook and a paleness under his tan turned his thin face into the edge of a knife. If anything, Kincaid had lost weight during the roundup, something not afflicting any of the others since they had slaughtered a few of the older, tougher cattle.

For all his joshing, John couldn't remember when he had eaten better. Texas Dunn was a good cook and with an entire herd to draw from, they had dined on steak more often than not during the past weeks. He and the other cowboys had burned off the food quickly, but Kincaid hadn't been as active. And he had grown thinner, much thinner now that John reflected on it.

"Get the herd to the Flying K's south pastures, then we'll have a little celebration," Kincaid finished, "before you boys head on into town for the social!"

He jumped from the stump and almost fell. John caught him, marveling at how paper thin and frail the man seemed. Kincaid pulled back, as if fearing John would notice he was little more than skin and bones.

"Are you feeling well, Mr. Kincaid?" John asked, concerned.

"Don't ever say a thing like that to me. I am perfectly fine." Kincaid stormed off, leaving John confused. If a man felt poorly, there was no disgrace in admitting that.

John wandered back to sit beside Texas. The cook chewed on a plug of tobacco and spit accurately, hitting a patch of grass already brown with the juice.

"What's eating at you?" the cook asked.

"Mr. Kincaid. I asked how he was feeling, and he got real curt with me."

"Seems he isn't as spry as he was even a month back. I figured it was the strain of the roundup. It does that, sometimes."

"Seems to be more than strain, but you might be right."

"Who can say? I'm no expert on anything, 'cept shoveling food into my mouth. That's why I'm such a good cook." Texas went back to work using his knife to scrape a pot with stew caked to the inside.

"You might want to leave that—for starter on a new meal," John suggested. He jumped back in time to avoid a new spray of tobacco juice. Laughing, John went off. His mood darkened again when he saw Kincaid talking with his foreman. The way the sun caught him turned him into a walking corpse. John waited for Kincaid to leave before approaching the foreman.

"Bill, wanted to ask a question."

"Make it snappy. We've got a passel of things to do if we want to get the herd into pastures before Friday."

"It's about Mr. Kincaid. Does he seem, well, healthy?"

"The only thing you have to know is that he's your boss and pays your wages. It's none of your business how healthy he is. Do you get my meaning?"

"I didn't mean anything by it. Honest. I'm just concerned that—"

"If you don't have enough to keep you busy, I can find it. We only have—consarn it. Where's my watch?" Bill patted himself down, failing to find his pocket watch. He peered up at the sun from under the brim of his hat and made a quick estimate. "We're moving the herd in an hour. All wranglers, even you, Allen. Get your gear packed and be in the saddle." The foreman stalked off, still searching for his watch.

Knowing when he was butting his head against a stone wall, John went to roll his gear and prepare for the drive to the south pastures. The past weeks had been spent rounding up the herd and branding the new calves. Now they had to move the beeves in one large conglomeration to the Flying K for a week or two of fattening on sweet grass and what hay was left from winter fodder before beginning the drive to Cheyenne.

It was something new for him and he looked forward to it. John just wished Mr. Kincaid and the foreman weren't so touchy about the owner's health. A blind man could see Kincaid wasn't up to snuff.

Shrugging it off, John stowed his gear and saddled Old Sadie. The mare eyed him with her slightly disapproving glare, then submitted to him climbing into the saddle.

They fanned out behind the herd and, using lariats to swat bovine hindquarters, got the herd moving slowly in the desired direction. Bill rode everywhere, shouting and advising, cajoling and ordering. John did what he could to follow orders but his inexperience caused more than one of the other wranglers to join him to keep control. The balky beeves tried to sneak past him and he lacked the experience to stop them.

"Let 'em go, even for a minute," cautioned Cassidy, "and you'll have half the herd following. They're dumb brutes. And never let one start to run. Lasso it if you have to, bulldog it to the ground, do what you have to but don't let it run."

"Stampede, I know about them," John declared, though his only experience had been talking with Carver Norton. The man's vivid description of ten thousand tons of unstoppable cattle roaring down the trail had made quite an impression.

Cassidy nodded and returned to his own section of the herd. John's ability to keep the cattle within the body of the herd improved and he was almost sorry to see sundown come. It had been a long, hard day, and they were two or more days from reaching the Flying K, but he had begun to enjoy the work.

"Where is it? I had it here a minute ago!" Texas raged about, flinging pots and pans in all directions. The cook burrowed into the back of the chuck wagon and crawled back, empty-handed.

"What did you lose this time?" John called to the cook.

"My good knife. That blade cost me purty near twenty dollars and I've had it for as many years. It was here a minute ago. I had it in my hand. You saw me with it. I was cleaning out the stew pot with it." The cook roared around, hunting for his lost knife.

Texas cooled down and finally made do with another knife, one John promised to sharpen when they returned to the ranch. The wranglers sat in a wide half circle around the campfire as they ate. Texas stormed about, insulting them, making sure each had his fill. But the cook stopped and stared when he reached Jackson.

"You! You varmint! You sidewinder! You stole my knife!" Before the cowboy could say a word, Texas seized him by the shoulders and bodily lifted him to his feet. The cook shook him like a terrier with a rat. From the wrangler's belt fell a knife.

Texas' knife.

No one in the company failed to recognize it because Texas had used it every day of the roundup and had for years.

"Wait, you got it all wrong," protested Jackson. "I didn't steal it. I . . . I just borrowed it."

"I never lend my knife to nobody, especially a no account like you!"

"You're gettin' old, Texas," Jackson protested. "You lent it to me and forgot. I was going to give it back. Honest!"

"There's not an honest bone in your worthless body." Texas shook the cowboy even harder. When Jackson started for the six-shooter at his side, three others grabbed. One snarled Jackson's wrist. Another batted away the six-gun. The other's arms circled the man's body and dragged him away from the furious cook.

"What's going on?" Bill demanded. What's the ruckus about?"

"He stole my knife! I found it on him!" Texas grabbed for Jackson again but the others held him back.

"That's the cook's knife," Bill said, holding it up to get a better look at it in the campfire light. "What do you have to say about it, Jackson?"

"He gave it to me. I was going to return it but forgot. I got busy and—"

"I never—"

"Kangaroo Court!" went up the shout.

John stood and watched, not sure what was going on. He nudged Lou Cassidy and asked, "What are they talking about?"

"We're going to have a trial. It's not legal, not exactly, but no one in the Flying K outfit is allowed to steal. You know the rules. You saw them posted on the chuck house door. All of us agreed to follow them, even if we can't read."

John nodded. He remembered the list. No swearing or obscene gestures, no gambling, everybody shared in the chores, no stealing—those were the rules everyone in the outfit abided by. They worked so closely together, at the ranch and on roundup, they had to trust each other. What Jackson had done was a severe breach of etiquette.

Worse, he had betrayed his friends by stealing.

"What's to be done?" John asked.

"He'll get the chance to defend himself. Anyone who wants can question him. Then we all vote."

"We're all the jury? Mighty big jury, isn't it?"

"That's the only way to be sure everyone's heard and no one's feelings get hurt. Jackson might have a friend or two speak up for him. I surely won't. Never could tolerate the man. Never bathed regular. Fact is, I don't know that he didn't steal some tobacco from me right at the start of the roundup."

"Missing a bath or two's not a crime, though I admit preferring to ride upwind from him, myself," John said.

Jackson was placed in the middle of a circle. John heaved a sigh of relief he wasn't the one put there. Nothing but hostile eyes stared at the wrangler. Texas made his spiel about never loaning his precious knife and others agreed. But Jackson had hardly begun defending himself when Bill walked into the circle of light, carrying Jackson's gear.

The foreman dumped it out, spreading the blanket so the contents would be seen easily. The entire time, he never said a word. But Bill bent over and picked up a watch. He let it spin slowly in the firelight before tucking it into his vest pocket. Others scrambled forward to paw silently through the cornucopia revealed. Hardly a man came away without one or two items.

Not once was a word said.

John watched Jackson carefully and saw the color drain from the man's suntanned face when Bill showed the bedroll and all the purloined belongings. And he stopped his defense, standing sullenly with arms crossed. His lip curled into a sneer and he looked as if he hated the world.

"Reckon we've had time to ponder our decision," Bill said. His voice was low and soft but it carried. "You gents ready to vote?"

"Guilty!" cried Texas.

One by one, the wranglers around the circle voiced their verdict. John never hesitated when it came to his turn to add his guilty vote. The evidence was strong but the unrepentant expression on Jackson's face convicted him. He was as guilty as sin.

"It's unanimous," Bill said. "This Kangaroo Court finds you guilty. We can give you any number of punishments but—"

"Twenty lashes!" someone cried. "That's too good for him, but I want to give the first one. He stole my wife's picture!"

"But"—Bill plowed on, ignoring the outcry—"only one seems proper. Strip him of all his belongings except the clothes on his back."

"You can't do this! I own—"

"You own nothing but your life and duds," Bill said firmly. "The horses you ride belong to the Flying K. So does your saddle and other tack. The bedroll and your wages are forfeit. I'd recommend you start walking before we decide to take your boots."

"I'll get even for this. You can't do this to me. I'll get even with you all!"

Stony silence met the outbreak. In its way, the utter silence was more frightening than if the wranglers had returned the threats. Jackson spun and dashed from sight. For several seconds no one said a word, then Texas called, "Who wants seconds? We got plenty tonight of victuals, men."

Several lined up for the cook to ladle out more stew, but John had lost his appetite. He stared into the night after Jackson, wondering if the man was likely to make good on any of his threats.

Chapter Thirteen

"You surely did get all gussied up in your Sunday best for the hoedown. You thinking on finding yourself a filly tonight, John?" Lou Cassidy rocked back and laughed at John's obvious discomfort.

"There's nothing wrong with taking a bath more'n once a month," John said, trying to defend himself. He self-consciously adjusted his string tie and almost choked himself.

"You sure do stink purty," Texas Dunn chimed in. "Is that rose water?" The cook sniffed hard and shook his head. "It doesn't smell like it. More like you got into my cooking stores and dabbed some vanilla behind your ears."

"More like something from the bottom of your can of lard," offered another wrangler.

John sank back and listened to the ribald guesses as to why he smelled so different from the rest of them. He didn't much care if they joshed him a mite about the toilet water. He felt too good about getting into Chugwater and going to the hoedown. The work on the Flying K ranch had been hard these past weeks. The general roundup had gone as good as could be expected, but he thought it had gone well for him personally.

He had been allowed to ride with the wranglers. Working two jobs had taxed him sorely, but he didn't mind a little hard work. They had cut hay after getting the herd onto the south pastures and broke their backs moving it to the cattle. Grass would fatten up the beeves, but the hay would work faster. Sassy cattle would puff up the price Kincaid could ask for his herd at the Cheyenne City railhead.

And that made them all happy because Kincaid had promised a bonus if they were the first outfit to arrive. The first always got preferential treatment in shipping and price.

"Here we are, you galoots. Don't get into trouble. If you get tossed into the calaboose, you'll spend the night there," Bill warned. The wranglers let out a whoop of glee and bailed over the sides of the freight wagon, leaving behind John and the foreman.

"Go on," the foreman urged. "Or don't you have anything to do before the hoedown?"

"I don't drink and I don't gamble," John said, "but I've been doing some hard thinking."

"Don't hurt yourself. Get on out of the wagon. I don't want to see your ugly face until midnight, when the social is over." Seconds after John's feet touched Chugwater's dusty street, Bill snapped the reins and took off. The cowboys had speculated that their foreman had a sweetheart in town, but no one knew who it was. Not for certain, talk of Bill and the schoolmarm took on epic proportions.

John decided he had time to follow his idea for a spell. He went to the marshal's office and poked his head in the door. A balding man sat at the desk, a young girl of sixteen or seventeen standing in front of him with her head bowed and looking contrite.

"Marshal Lane?" John wasn't sure he had found the peace officer.

"I'm the fool who keeps getting elected. What can I do for you?" The marshal hesitated, seeing John's puzzled look. "This here is my daughter, Cara, if that's botherin' you. I'm not teaching her the business, just showing her the kind of men who get thrown into my jail so she'll know who to avoid when she gets older."

"I hope I'm not one of them." John tipped his hat to the young woman, who uneasily shifted from foot to foot but didn't say a word. She watched him out of the corner of her eye as if he might turn into a rattlesnake and bite her.

"You don't have the look. What can I do for you?" he repeated, obviously more inclined to lecture his daughter than to waste time with a ranch hand.

"I wondered if you have a file of wanted posters?" John quickly explained what had happened with Jackson and how he might be involved in more than the petty thieving around camp.

"How do you figure he's tied in with the cattle rustlers?" Marshal Lane glanced up at his daughter, then fumbled for a thick file of wanted posters in his bottom desk drawer.

"I have some suspicions," John said, remembering he had not seen clearly the face of the man Sam Yarbrough met. "I got the idea Jackson might be telling his friends when best to rustle Flying K cattle. The Square 7 brand isn't one anybody on the spread knows."

"Square 7? Never heard of it, either," the marshal said. He dropped the file on his desk. "Have a look. Tell me if you find anything interesting."

John quickly leafed through the posters. He found two that might have been Jackson, though neither had the man's name emblazoned along the top. But he knew many outlaws used summer names, taking aliases and then moving on if anyone discovered their real identities.

"You find your Mr. Jackson?"

"Might have. The pictures don't do him justice." John turned the pictures this way and that but could not be positive about either one.

"Who might this Henry Jackson have been telling about Flying K cattle so's they could rustle them when you weren't looking?" The question came smooth and easy, but John felt the tension behind it. The marshal had been pilloried by the cattle growers' association for not doing more to stop the rustlers. This might be the break he needed to put an end to their depredations.

"Wouldn't be right saying, not without real proof," John said. "Sorry I can't be more certain." He put the posters back into the stack and returned it to the marshal.

"I'm sorry, too," the lawman said. "Nothing I'd like more than to put those owlhoots behind bars." He stuffed his posters back into the drawer and closed it with a bang. "Go enjoy yourself at the hoedown," Marshal Lane said. "Me and the missus and the young'n will be over later. Won't we, Cara?" The pointed way the lawman spoke told John he had interrupted a family argument.

John hastily thanked the lawman for his time and went outside. The sun had set and left behind a coolness to the air characteristic of the high mountains. Trying not to appear too anxious but still walking quicker than usual, John made his way down the street to the lodge hall. The doors were propped open and all the furniture inside had been pushed back against the walls to make a dance floor. A sizable number of people had already gathered, but John hardly noticed them. His eyes fixed on the most beautiful woman in the room.

Lisa Holcroft stood beside her father, hand resting on his shoulder. He was seated in a sturdy chair and looked like he was some kind of royalty holding court. The elder Holcroft spoke with several prosperous looking men gathered in a half circle in front of him, possibly lodge brothers. John gathered his courage and went inside.

Blue eyes fixed on him immediately. Lisa Holcroft smiled winningly and motioned for him to join her. John needed no second invitation.

"Mr. Allen," she greeted, her voice as soft and beautiful as wind through the pines, "how nice that you could come into town for the social."

"Is this the young man, Lisa?" Charles Holcroft forced himself to stand. He thrust out his hand. "I owe you my life, sir. Thanks are hardly good enough."

"A dance with your daughter would be payment enough," John said before he realized what he was saying.

For a moment Holcroft was taken aback. Then he laughed. "You've got fire, son. But then it stands to reason. You wrested me from rustlers and that took a fair amount of grit. However, I cannot grant that wish."

"Sorry," John started. He felt a hot flush coming to his face and he knew he had overstepped the bounds of politeness by asking.

"No, you misunderstand. It is my daughter's decision to make, not mine. Even if she will not dance with you, please accept my thanks and my sincere offer to come work on the Rolling H. I can always use bold, brave men like you."

"You want me as a wrangler?" John's eyebrows shot up in surprise.

"Why not? I'll match anything Warner is paying, and add five dollars a month to it."

"That's mighty generous, but I already get more than you pay top hands," John said, knowing what Carver Norton got paid. This rocked Holcroft a mite.

"It figures. That scoundrel Warner knows good men when he sees 'em—and how to keep them."

"If you will not accept Papa's offer of a job, then it is my duty to repay you with the dance. Sir?" Lisa held out her arm. John was slow in taking it, not realizing she actually was granting permission for him to escort her. Only when Holcroft cleared his throat and looked hard at him did John find the courage to take her arm and escort her onto the dance floor. Even then, they waited for three other couples to join them for a proper number of couples to give the band something worth doing. The band started playing as the caller began his sprightly square dance calling.

John was never sure exactly how long the dance lasted. He remembered swinging to and fro and around with Lisa on his arm. They separated and came together in a Texas Star and then it was over.

"That's the finest dance I've ever had," he told her. "Having a lovely partner does a lot to enhance my footwork."

"And it certainly seems to set your tongue to wagging," she said, smiling brightly. Before John could ask for a second dance, he felt a shoulder move him to one side.

Whitey Yarbrough interposed himself between them.

"This dance is mine, Lisa," the Rolling H foreman said, too loudly for John's taste. Yarbrough shot John a sour look, then turned his back to him.

"It's been a pleasure, Miss Holcroft," John said, gracefully accepting the woman's decision to dance with her betrothed. Still, it galled him to see her dancing with the man.

John stood and stared at them, not aware he did so. He jumped when a hand on his arm drew him away from the dance floor.

"Join me in a drink, Mr. Allen." Charles Holcroft wobbled a little as he walked. "She's a good dancer, isn't she?"

"Yes, sir!"

"There's so much of her mother in her. I don't think it except at times like these. Lisa hasn't been smiling much or laughing, for all that. She's been working too hard tending an old man and his wound." Holcroft tapped his chest.

"Other than a little weakness, you seem well recovered, sir." John remembered what Carver had said about the doctor pulling the bullet out from alongside a rib. "Chest wounds are always serious, and I heard tell you had a cracked rib along with it."

"That I did. Don't remember much of what happened. The doctor said that is not unusual." Holcroft heaved a sigh and signalled for two drinks. John started to push it away when Holcroft said, "I trust you won't mind some sarsaparilla. The cursed doctor warned me against drinking anything harder."

"This suits me just fine, sir." John sipped at the root beer and turned slightly so he could watch Lisa from the corner of his eye without appearing too forward.

"She's quite a sight to behold, isn't she?"

"Sir?"

"My daughter," Holcroft said irritably. "You're not blind, man. I wish she'd hurry and marry Whitey. What with the rustlers and running the Rolling H, it's all wearing me down something fierce. I need to rest. I need to retire."

"A young man like you, sir? Ridiculous." John worried over Holcroft's insistence on his daughter marrying Yarbrough.

"I'll have a few good years left, but I want to turn over operations to a son. A son-in-law," he corrected.

"How well do you know Whitey Yarbrough?"

"How well? He's worked for me these past six years, starting as a greenhorn and working his way up to foreman. I know him as well as I do any man."

"What would you say if there was proof his brother was tied in with the rustlers?"

"Sam? Nonsense. Sam's a hothead but he is as honest as the day is long. I will not listen to any slander of him."

"Might not be slander," John said carefully. "Do you know one of Mr. Kincaid's wranglers by the name of Henry Jackson?"

Holcroft shook his head.

"Jackson was run out of camp for petty thieving, but I think I saw him meet Sam Yarbrough during the roundup. If Jackson waited for just the right time, he could tell Yarbrough when and where to raid the herd."

"I'm hearing too many 'ifs' and 'I thinks' in your speech, Mr. Allen. Are you certain this Jackson is a rustler?"

"I found two wanted posters in the marshal's files. Either might be him under a different name."

"Names are like snakeskins out West. You shed one and move on with another," Holcroft said. He frowned as he thought. He took a long drink and put down the empty glass before saying, "I'll look at the marshal's posters. I cannot believe Sam is involved in anything illegal, much less stealing my beeves."

"Do you know who owns the Square 7 ranch?"

"Square 7? Never heard of it." Holcroft waved to his daughter and Yarbrough, urging them to come over. "Mr. Allen asked about the Square 7. Do you know anything about who owns it, Whitey?"

"No, sir, I don't. Is it important?" Yarbrough stared at John with an unfathomable expression.

"Reckon not," Holcroft said. "At least not as important as my daughter permitting me to have one dance."

"Papa, are you up to it?"

"I should say so!" Holcroft took Lisa's arm and let her steer him across the floor. Yarbrough watched for a moment, glared at John, then left the lodge hall. John watched father and daughter dance, realizing her grace lent itself well to any partner. She made even an injured Holcroft appear light on his feet.

"I'm winded," Holcroft said, returning to stand beside John after the band wound down their lively reel.

"I trust Miss Holcroft isn't too tuckered out. Would you permit me one more dance?" John startled himself with the request. He wasn't usually this bold but something about the woman brought it out of him. She was a beauty to behold but there was more that spoke to him.

"Why, since Whitey's gone off without so much as a good-bye, I see no reason why not. Wherever did he go?" Lisa looked around for him, stamped her foot impatiently, then offered her arm to John once more.

John didn't bother with answering her as he led her back onto the dance floor. Let her think what she wanted of her fiancé. All John knew was that it was the best night of his life.

Chapter Fourteen

"Please, Mr. Allen, I need to catch my breath." Lisa Holcroft put her hand to her throat and then fanned herself a moment.

"It is hot inside. Perhaps you'd care to step outside for a moment? The night's not too cool for you, I hope."

"I've lived in Wyoming all my life," she said, a smile curling her lips. "I'm aware of the weather—and I am no hothouse flower."

She shifted her skirts and preceded John outside into the crisp summer night. They found chairs at the end of the porch in front of the lodge hall, remaining within view of anyone inside. The people coming and going cast sidelong glances at them but there was nothing improper in simply sitting in public and talking. John made sure of that. The last thing he wanted to do was besmirch Lisa's good name.

"Do you know where Whitey went?" she asked unexpectedly.

"Why, no, I don't." He held his tongue, not adding that he was glad the Rolling H foreman had taken off like a scalded dog. John frowned a little, remembering the reason why Yarbrough had hightailed it. Charles Holcroft had been defending Sam Yarbrough's reputation.

"I worry about him. He works hard, but he often goes off for days on end and no one knows where he is."

"Not even his brother?"

"Strange that you keep mentioning Sam. I trust this has nothing to do with the set-to on the train. I don't like the notion of you two feuding, and I do wish you'd take the time to get to know Whitey better. He really is a good man." Lisa fell silent but John heard more in the quiet than in her words. She wanted to say more.

Lisa finally turned and clasped John's hands in hers. "Would you do me a favor, John?"

"Anything," he said, realizing she had called him by his given name rather the more formal "Mr. Allen."

"Please go find what Whitey is up to. He wanders off and won't tell me what he does." Her bright blue eyes stared imploringly at John. He melted inside.

"This might pose some, uh, problem if, uh—"

"I want to know where he goes, John. You don't need to cover it in sugar if he's with another woman. I doubt that's where he is, but I'd want to know, regardless. And I don't think you would lie to me about it, either."

"I might not be the best one to find out for you."

"You're an honest man. I see it in your eyes—and everyone else says so too."

"Who's 'everyone else?' "

"Reckon you caught me sayin' good things about you, John. I promise not to do it again," Carver Norton said, coming from inside the lodge hall. "Your pa's getting real antsy over you being out here, Miss Holcroft," the wrangler said. "Besides that, I might have two left feet but I'd be real obliged to you if you'd see fit to dance with me."

"Very well, Mr. Norton," she said, rising. She reached out and touched John's hand lightly again. "Thank you," Lisa said and then whirled away on Carver's proffered arm.

John sank back in the hard chair. The night suddenly turned colder and lonelier. He didn't know what to do. He had promised, but what would he really tell her if he found Yarbrough was sneaking out to see a prostitute? Or even worse, what if he and his brother were involved in rustling? John had to consider the very real possibility that the Rolling H foreman had been startled at hearing mention of the Square 7 brand because he had something to do with it.

Or was he being overly protective of his younger sibling as so many others claimed? Yarbrough might know of Sam's involvement but be hiding it because of duty to a wayward brother. Whatever proved to be the truth, John knew he had to tell Lisa because he had promised. For once, for Lisa's sake, he hoped that his worst suspicions about the Yarbrough brothers were all wet.

Grumbling to himself, he pushed to his feet and walked to the middle of Chugwater's main street. Looking up and down the dusty track he saw few people stirring. Most everyone in town crowded into the lodge hall for the hoedown—everyone but Yarbrough.

Not liking it but seeing no other course, John set off to look into every saloon along the main street. It took only ten minutes to find Yarbrough in a gambling emporium, sitting with his back to the room. The four men seated around the table with Whitey exchanged glances often and made curious gestures. John saw all this in a few seconds, and wondered why Yarbrough remained in a crooked game. It didn't take a professional gambler to realize who the sucker was at this table.

"What can I get you, cowboy?" the barkeep asked.

"Cider," John said. The barkeep's lip curled in contempt and his mustache twitched but he put a filled glass in front of John.

"Anything else?" The barkeep used a dirty rag to wipe off shot glasses as he talked.

"I wanted to talk with Whitey, but I see he's in a big game with those gents."

The barkeep snorted in disgust. "You might call it a game."

"But not the way Whitey plays, is that it?" John sipped at the cider and made a face. He had been given hard cider.

"It's pretty bad when even a cowpoke walking in can see what's happening. He surely does lose big, and not only to those four."

"How big can his losses be? He's only a top hand and couldn't make more than fifty a month."

"Fifty? He loses that much in a single hand, but his credit is good. He's more than a top hand or even foreman at a big ranch. Yarbrough's going to inherit all of Holcroft's money when he marries. That's why he's given any amount of credit, no matter how terrible he bets."

"Debts real big?" John wasn't sure if this was something to tell Lisa. She had wanted to know where her fiancé went, but this seemed to be Yarbrough's private matter and not anything the woman ought to hear.

"Yes and no. He runs up a big tab, then pays it off. Maybe he hits it rich in some other casino and uses the winnings to pay off here. I don't know and I don't ask. I just sell 'em tarantula juice when they ask for it." The way the bartender spoke told John he was being given advice—to clear out and mind his own business.

John half turned and saw that Yarbrough had spotted him. The foreman started to push his cards to the center of the table but the others in the game would have none of it. They had yet to milk him for every last cent.

Yarbrough argued a few minutes with them, then accepted a new deal. He kept looking over his shoulder at

John, shooting him cold glares. John considered telling Yarbrough why he had followed him into the casino, then decided against it. He had made no promises to Lisa about secrecy, but had he really found out anything important about her fiancé?

Not much, he decided. And it certainly wasn't anything he could take to a jury. Yarbrough gambled. So did many men in Wyoming. If Charles Holcroft had rules similar to those Kincaid had posted, gambling on the Rolling H wasn't permitted. A man with a yen to bet a few dollars on the turn of the cards would find it easy in a Chugwater casino. If anything, this showed Yarbrough's respect for Holcroft's rules rather than the opposite.

John pushed away from the bar, leaving most of his hard cider untouched. He stepped into the street and shivered as a blast of cold wind whipped down off the mountains. Riding the range, alone and dependant on no one, appealed greatly to him. Only when he got involved with others did his troubles mount.

John heaved a deep sigh. Maybe Carver had been right back on the train. Maybe he wasn't cut out to be anything but a drifter, never content to stay in one place too long. But looking at the dark hulks of mountains all around and drinking in the fresh air said something different to John.

"Home," he muttered. This felt like home more than any other place he had ever been. St. Louis had not been home, not after his parents died. And the Nebraska coal mines had never been home. Every morning when he vanished into the pits, he had vowed it would be his last trip, that he would find a better job and place to live.

He loved working cattle and he loved Wyoming.

John knew what it would take to make things perfect, but one thing wasn't likely to happen. Lisa was spoken for.

Lost in his musing about life and love, John wasn't paying attention and bumped into a man. Stepping back, he quickly apologized. The words caught in his throat when he saw Sam Yarbrough.

"You!" Yarbrough cried. "Everywhere I turn, you're there messin' up everything."

The man's hand went for the six-shooter holstered at his hip. John put up his hands, as if to push Yarbrough back.

"I'm not armed. I don't wear a hogleg."

"You're nothing but a coward, always refusing to fight me. You backed down out on the range. You can't fight like a man."

"I gave you a fair chance on the train," John said, his hands clenching. "It wasn't my fault out on the range. Your brother's the one who backed down, but I don't see why we can't have this out here and now."

"I'm game," Yarbrough shouted. He pushed back his hat and rolled up his sleeves. John noted Yarbrough made no move to take off the six-shooter. That didn't worry him much. He was confident enough of his own pugilistic skills to think he could keep Yarbrough from going for the gun if the fight went against him.

When the fight went against Yarbrough, John amended. He had watched Yarbrough and Lou Cassidy have it out and knew Yarbrough wasn't much of a boxer. All he had to do was avoid punching to the body and he would be an easy victor over the Rolling H foreman's brother.

John pushed back his sleeves, giving no thought to ruining his good duds. He lifted his fists and judged distances.

"I'm ready, Yarbrough. Anytime you want to start, go on."

"I'll destroy you," Yarbrough cried, rushing forward. He wasn't going to box, he intended to catch John in a backbreaking hug and end the contest in a hurry. John danced away and let fly with two quick punches. The first opened a small crescent under Yarbrough's left eye. The other rocked his head back as it rolled off the man's temple.

"You know Henry Jackson?" John asked as he circled. "You and him in cahoots?"

"What are you saying?" A wild look came to Yarbrough's face. He made another clumsy attack. John held his ground and got in another solid punch to the man's eye. Knuckles throbbing, John knew he had to keep punching at Yarbrough's face. His rock-hard gut would break only fingers.

"Nothing. Just wondering if you two were partners in rustling cattle." John ducked a hard swing and moved in, fists flying. He repeatedly punched into Yarbrough's belly, feeling the stony wall beginning to weaken. John's hands ached but he knew better than to retreat once he got this close. He kept swinging until Yarbrough backed away.

Staggered, bloody, Yarbrough's expression turned wild.

"What's going on? You two stop it," the marshal called. John saw the lawman striding briskly across the street. Someone at the hoedown must have seen the fight and told the marshal.

Yarbrough looked left and right, then pulled down his hat and bolted, running from the lawman.

John dropped his guard and watched Yarbrough run like a hare chased by a hound. It was hard to figure why he was so afraid of the lawman—unless he had a guilty conscience.

Chapter Fifteen

John Allen rubbed his knuckles against his pants, then stopped, worrying about getting blood on them. He hadn't skinned himself up badly but he wanted to keep his good change of clothes looking nice. The marshal kept on walking, on his way to some other problem in Chugwater. He didn't even glance in John's direction as he passed.

Sam Yarbrough had retreated so fast only a memory was left. John looked for the man but he had already left town. Returning to the hoedown after the futile search, John saw Bill Diamond sitting on the broad wooden porch in front of the lodge hall.

"Come on over and set a spell, John," the foreman urged. He patted the wood plank beside him in invitation.

"I need to talk," John said.

"Reckon that makes a pair of us. I heard tell how you and Miss Holcroft were dancing up a storm. Everyone's buzzing about it."

"It doesn't mean a thing," John said, a flush rising. He was glad it was dark outside and the foreman couldn't see his expression clearly.

"Dangerous territory to explore, another man's woman," Bill said.

"I've found some other dangerous territory." John launched into his speculation about Sam Yarbrough but left out what he had discovered about Whitey Yarbrough's out of control gambling. A man's vices were his own unless they got too big and bothered other folks. John was still wrestling with whether he ought to tell Lisa about the big gambling losses when a small commotion at the lodge door pulled his attention.

"Evening all," called Charles Holcroft. His daughter helped the Rolling H rancher from the lodge, her arm around his waist to steady him. But John found himself staring rudely at Lisa. She was about the most beautiful woman he had ever seen.

She smiled brightly, made a move as if to come over to speak with him, then heeded her father's call to help him into a buggy waiting in front of the lodge. Lisa waved to John and smiled shyly as she and her father drove off, vanishing into the dark night far too soon. John heaved a sigh.

"That's the kind of thing that gets a man's head

blown off," Bill said. "Nothing but trouble if you rile Sam or Whitey." Bill worked on rolling a cigarette. His fingers nimbly spun the rolling paper, then held it in a steady grip as he added the tobacco. He licked the side, twisted and had himself a smoke in seconds. He lit up and took a deep puff before continuing with his unwanted advice. "Truth is, Sam's always looking for a dog to kick. Mean. Real mean through and through."

"I'm not afraid of him," John said. He had beaten Sam Yarbrough in a fair fight twice.

"From the look of your knuckles, that's probably true. Remember, John, Sam's the kind to reach for his six-shooter. If you just happen to be in his sights, I'm not sure he'd much care you weren't toting a six-gun of your own."

"What about him being behind the rustling?"

"It could happen the way you claim," Bill admitted. "Never did trust Henry Jackson much, and him being in cahoots with the rustlers is something he would do. Can't rightly say it's Sam Yarbrough."

"What about Whitey?"

This caused Bill's eyes to widen. "You accusing him of being a rustler?" The Flying K foreman laughed. "He's got too much to lose. When he marries Miss Holcroft, he'll be in line to inherit the entire Rolling H. What's a few lousy stolen beeves compared to a couple thousand legitimate ones?"

"Maybe he doesn't want to be tied down. Might be he thinks about moving on more than settling down."

"I've heard stranger things," Bill allowed. "Impending marriage makes some men act peculiar."

Again John held his tongue about Whitey Yarbrough and his wild gambling—and he wasn't sure why. Perhaps it was his innate good nature not to accuse someone without facts.

Or maybe it was something more. John could not deny how irked he was about Lisa being betrothed to Whitey. She deserved better than a man with a pile of gambling losses, even if he did cover them somehow. Still, other tiny pieces of the puzzle refused to drop into place for him.

Bill pulled out his watch and opened the case. He peered at it and said, "Round up the boys. It's time to head back to the Flying K 'fore any of them get into real trouble."

"All right." John paused for a moment, turned and asked, "Did Mr. Kincaid come to the hoedown? I didn't see him earlier."

"He wasn't feeling up to it." The way the foreman turned cautious told John he was treading on quicksand. Going on the roundup had made Kincaid as limp as a worn-out fiddle string. He dropped the inquiry and went to tell Texas Dunn to get on out to the wagon. If the cook knew, everyone else would in a few minutes.

The cowboys sang boisterously on the way back to the Flying K, but John simply sat and thought hard about Whitey Yarbrough and his brother—and Lisa Holcroft. Mostly, he thought of the midnight-haired beauty.

Before he realized it, Bill shouted, "Everybody out and hit the rack. We've got a full day ahead of us tomorrow."

John groaned as he stretched cramped muscles. He jumped to the ground, landing beside Texas.

"Go on over and see if Mr. Kincaid wants anything to eat," the foreman told the cook. "His light's still on. Don't reckon he fixed himself anything for dinner. You know how he is."

"I surely do. Ever since the missus died, he skips meals 'less I remind him."

"Maybe it's his way of protecting himself from your poisoning," John suggested.

"You get on out of here," Texas said, taking a wild, playful swing at John. The cook hurried to the ranch house and rapped on the door. John turned toward the bunkhouse but stopped when he heard the cook shout for help.

John, Bill and two other wranglers dashed for the house and went inside. John paused just inside the door. Bill and Texas stood beside Kincaid, who had slumped over his writing desk.

"Is he dead?" John choked out the words.

"He's still breathin' but he's in a bad way," Texas said.

"John, saddle up and get back into town. Fetch the doc and get him out here pronto."

John never hesitated. He turned and dashed from the ranch house, intent on getting help. He wasn't the best rider but he knew the foreman trusted him to carry out the duty without any back talk or delay.

Running to the corral, John saw Old Sadie quietly munching hay. Beside her Arroyo pawed at the ground, switching hooves as he bicycled in his way. John knew it would take forever reaching Chugwater on the mare. He threw his saddle over Arroyo's back. The powerful strawberry roan tried to rear but John held the horse in check.

Swinging into the saddle, John felt the horse settle down. Arroyo might not be fully broken but he was a better choice for a fast trip into town. John put his heels into the roan's flanks. Arroyo rocketed away.

John galloped hard down the road, then realized he couldn't go more than a couple miles at this pace. Even a strong horse flagged quickly. Pushing down the urgency he felt, John began thinking. He tugged at Arroyo's reins and got the horse off the road, which meandered around. He could cut miles off the trip and get back that much faster by striking out cross-country.

He had to fight Arroyo at every turn. The horse had a mind of his own and wanted to chase this way and that. And this battle between man and mount finally betrayed John. He got lost.

A sinking feeling hit him when he looked up after almost an hour of riding and realized he didn't rightly know where he was. Arroyo had subtly edged off course at every hint of inattention by his rider.

"Mr. Kincaid's going to die if I don't find the road into town," John said, trying to settle his rising panic. Bill had sent him to fetch the doctor because he trusted him. John couldn't betray that faith or let his boss suffer any more.

He steadied Arroyo, then rode the roan to the top of a rise. He heaved a sigh of relief when he recognized a watering hole. Less than ten miles from town, he knew where he was and how to get into Chugwater in jig time. But John held back Arroyo when he saw Sam Yarbrough. John didn't want to tangle with Yarbrough right now—and he remembered the warning Bill had given.

Yarbrough was a hothead and might be inclined to shoot first if he came across a lone enemy. The watering hole was isolated and catching a lead slug in his gut would do nothing for his disposition or to help Kincaid.

John started to circle the hole when he unexpectedly came upon another rider. He sucked in his breath as he recognized the rider as the same person John had seen Yarbrough arguing with a week earlier.

"Who—?" John started. Then he recognized who had ridden out to meet Sam Yarbrough.

"You were in my pa's office earlier tonight. What are you doing here?" the marshal's daughter demanded. She pushed back the tall Stetson she wore like a man. Cara Lane wore a man's clothing but there was nothing manly about her.

"What's going on?" Yarbrough shouted. He rode over and moved beside Cara. "He bothering you?" Yarbrough reached for his six-shooter but Cara grabbed his wrist.

"No, Sam, don't. You knew we'd be found out sooner or later."

"Found out?" John frowned. He wasn't sure what was going on. Then he realized he had interrupted a lover's tryst.

"I love her," Yarbrough said belligerently. "And nothing you can do or say will change that."

"Sam, wait. Why are you out here?" the woman asked John.

He quickly explained Kincaid's problem, finishing, "I didn't intend spying on you, though I must have seen you before. Were you arguing a couple weeks back?"

"I'm afraid we were. We had a spat," Cara said.

"It's like we always do," Yarbrough supplied. "I want to marry her but she's a'feared of what her pa might do."

"You are a good man, Sam Yarbrough," she said firmly. "Pa won't say no if we both ask him."

Yarbrough laughed harshly. "He's never liked me, and he'd horsewhip me if he found I was courting his oldest daughter."

"He'll come around, given enough time to get used to it," Cara said. She turned toward John. "You aren't going to tell him, are you?"

John's mind raced. He had no quarrel with Yarbrough, not really. And he had no reason to get Cara in Dutch with her pa.

"All I'm interested in is getting the doctor back to the Flying K. Mr. Kincaid's dying."

"Very well," the woman said. "Sam will show you the fastest way back to town, since his horse is stronger than mine. In return, you won't mention seeing us together."

"You might consider letting your father know how you feel," John advised. "One day someone is going to see you together who doesn't have a desperate ride ahead of him."

"We shall," she said. "We need to ease into it. My pa's been marshal so long he thinks he can tell everyone what to do, even his own daughter."

"Sometimes it's best to just jump into the pond, no matter how cold the water," John said.

"Don't go mouthing off," Yarbrough said. John saw the man's anger rising.

"I agree to say nothing about seeing you and Miss Lane together, but we *have* to get into Chugwater. Mr. Kincaid needs the doctor bad!"

"Come on." Yarbrough bent over, gave Cara a quick kiss, shot a defiant look at John, then wheeled his horse and took off at a brisk trot. John let Arroyo have his head and the roan quickly overtook Yarbrough. They rode side by side for two miles, saying nothing. But the quiet wore on John and questions bubbled up he had to ask.

"Tell me, Yarbrough, how much does your brother owe in gambling debts?"

"What? Whitey? Nothing. He doesn't owe anybody anything."

"I saw how he gambles. He's terrible at it. Four professional gamblers were fleecing him like a spring lamb. It doesn't take many bad poker hands for a man to be deep in debt."

"He doesn't owe anything," Yarbrough insisted. "He

always pays off what he loses. Might take a day or two, but he always pays his due."

"How?" The question escaped John's lips before he realized he had uttered it.

"He gets good money. Fifty a month as foreman."

John had seen Whitey Yarbrough lose that much in a single hand of five card stud. The bartender might have been right that Yarbrough won in other casinos, but that didn't seem too likely. A man betting as wildly as Whitey had done wasn't going to win much anywhere else. He was no better than a man dying of thirst in the desert, vultures circling overhead. Every real gambler in Chugwater would circle the table, waiting for a chance to pluck a few more dollars from Whitey's hand.

"Does he take money from Lisa Holcroft?"

"What?" Yarbrough bellowed. "Are you plaguing me for any good reason other than you don't like me? My brother'd never take money from a woman."

"And her father would never offer it." John had talked enough with Charles Holcroft to know he was a self-made man. And men like the Rolling H's owner figured others could make their own stake, as he had done. Even considering Whitey Yarbrough as a potential son-in-law, Holcroft would never pay off gambling debts. If anything, that would make him drive the foreman off the spread. Holcroft didn't seem to be a man who cottoned much to weakness in others.

Yarbrough grunted but didn't answer directly. From the way he hunched forward, John knew he was right in his appraisal of Holcroft. Before he knew it, they reached the end of Chugwater's main street.

"Where do I find the doctor?" John asked. He had wandered around the town but had not seen the saw-bones' office. Yarbrough pointed and John thanked him. As he rode off, Yarbrough called after him.

"Don't forget your promise."

"I'm an honorable man," John shot back. "I keep my word." He dropped to the ground and rushed to the stairs leading to the second floor office. He pounded long minutes before the doctor came to the door, rubbing sleep from his eyes.

"Emergency," John cried. He explained quickly as the doctor dressed.

The doctor eschewed his buggy in favor of a saddled horse to speed their return to the Flying K. Riding hard, John and the doctor got back to the ranch house just before dawn.

Kincaid had died a few minutes after John had left to get the doctor.

Chapter Sixteen

John Allen stood and stared at Bill Diamond as the foreman repeated it.

"He died right after you rode out, John. I'm sorry. Your trip wasn't needed."

"But—" John tried to speak but the words jumbled in his throat. If he had been faster, if he hadn't gotten lost, the tryst between Marshall Lane's daughter and Sam Yarbrough, the time getting back—if he had been faster.

"It wouldn't have been your fault, even if you'd gone faster 'n lightning," Texas Dunn said, clapping John on the shoulder. "You did the best you could, and it wasn't good enough. Nothing any of us could do was good enough."

"They are right," the doctor said, closing his bag. "Don't go blaming yourself. Even if we had gotten back while Warner was alive, there's not much I could have done. He had a heart attack, probably brought on by his weakened condition."

"We got other problems to contend with," the foreman said. "Get the men rounded up. Doc, you want to stay and listen to this—as witness?"

"The will?" The doctor took the folded paper from Bill's hand and scanned it quickly. "I'm no lawyer but this looks all right and proper, done up in legalese. You do what you have to and I'll report it to the marshal."

John sat on the edge of the porch, still stunned at the rancher's sudden death. Kincaid hadn't looked fit for weeks, but John had not thought the man was going to up and die suddenly like this. It didn't seem fair. They had worked for Kincaid and rounded up more cattle than anyone would have thought. John felt abandoned—and worse.

His future evaporated with Kincaid's death. What was he going to do now?

"Listen up, men," Bill called. "You've all heard about Mr. Kincaid. The doctor said it was his heart, that there was nothing anyone could do." The foreman glanced in John's direction, as if to reassure him. John still didn't feel any better.

"What's going to happen now? We got the whole danged herd down in the south pasture," Cassidy asked.

"This is Mr. Kincaid's will. Texas and I found it on Mr. Kincaid's desk. Seemed he was going over it, as if he knew his days were numbered. You all know he had no living kin. His wife and kids died years back." Bill unfurled the legal paper and began reading.

For a few seconds, John wasn't sure what he heard. Then he stood and moved closer, listening hard.

"So that's it," Bill finished. "The Flying K is to be divvied up amongst us as outlined, according to how long you've worked here and how much you're earning in salary."

John's mind boiled with the numbers. Few on the ranch had been here long. Kincaid had been hiring greenhorns because he didn't have much operating cash. Fact was, Texas, Bill and Cassidy were the only ones who had been with the Flying K longer than two years—and because he worked two jobs John earned more than any other on the spread save for Bill.

His share of the Flying K would be one of the largest. He shook his head as he tried to understand what had happened. John Allen, ranch owner. Part of the herd was his and a considerable part of the profits.

He was rich!

"There's a problem with this, men," Bill said. "We'll have to do some tallying but the Flying K has considerable debts levied against it."

"You mean we're not rich, that by dying Kincaid put us in *debt*? I can do that on my own!"

John didn't know who spoke but the response rippling through the gathered wranglers combined both laughter and indignation.

"We just don't know, not yet," the foreman said.

"I don't want any part of it if I'm going to be owing bankers. Let 'em starve, I say. They never treated me or mine very well, and they're not getting my wages!"

"No one's forcing you to take a share," the doctor spoke up. "You can turn it down, but that means who- ever does accept their shares in the Flying K will have bigger pieces of the pie."

"Count me out!" several cried in unison.

John's mind began turning over numbers in earnest now. He had tried to put an informal set of books into order out on the roundup but had failed because he knew too little of the Flying K's resources.

He jumped up next to Bill and said loudly, "Men, we might not get rich but we can do all right if—"

"Buy me out, John, if you think this is such a good deal."

"Very well," John shot back. "I'll pay every man wanting it double his current salary if you stick with the Flying K until we get the herd to Cheyenne—but you have to sign over to me your share in the ranch."

"You'll guarantee *twice* our salaries *and* take on any debt left by Mr. Kincaid?"

"That's what I will do," John said, heart beating rap- idly. He knew he might be mortgaging his future. He also knew he might be guaranteeing it. "I don't want any of you to take me up on this offer unless you're serious."

"I'm no rancher. What would I do with a part interest in the Flying K?" one wrangler asked. "I do better working for someone so I can depend on a wage."

"Bill, will you help on this? You stand to be the largest owner of the ranch."

"John, if you want to take on the headaches of this place, I'll be the first to sign over my portion to you. Besides," he said, smiling, "I surely can use a hundred dollars a month."

"I don't want to cheat anyone," John said hurriedly.

"Then you won't mind giving us our current salary in advance with the other half after we deliver the herd?" This came from Cassidy.

"Seems fair," Texas cut in, rubbing his bearded chin. "That way, no matter what happens, we're not out a season's pay."

John took a deep breath and knew he had to fish or cut bait.

"I'll do it. Your entire season's salary now, an equal amount after we get to Cheyenne City and sell the herd."

The men let out a whoop of delight and cheered for five minutes. John let them slap him on the back and pump his hand. He hardly noticed since he was in a state of shock. And he was even more stunned by the time he found the Flying K records and meticulously went over the long columns of numbers.

And by the time he finished, a long line of creditors filed into the ranch house demanding their due. John spent the better part of the day and long into the night arguing with them, cajoling, negotiating and signing new promissory notes to keep the ranch going, at least for a few more weeks.

He fell asleep at the very desk where Kincaid had died, only to jerk awake when he heard boots crossing the wooden floor. John saw Bill standing in front of him.

"It's a bother, isn't it?"

"Being the owner of the Flying K?" John shook his head. "I never realized what I was getting into."

"You can just ride on out. I wouldn't hold it against you, and I doubt the men would either. You made mighty generous offers to them."

"I'm not turning tail and running. I stand by my word, though—"

"How much do you owe the creditors?"

"Adding in the wages I promised, just about a thousand dollars. I asked the banker for a loan and he refused. He said he wouldn't give it to Mr. Kincaid, who was a lodge brother, and he wasn't about to give it to a kid still wet behind the ears." John shook his head. "I haven't thought of myself that way since I was fourteen."

"What are you going to do?"

For a moment, John had no answer. Then an idea came to him. He said, "I'm going to be enterprising." Slamming shut the ledger book, he pushed past the foreman and went to saddle Arroyo. He had a long ride ahead of him before the sun set on the Flying K for good.

John wiped his lips, realizing how dry his mouth had turned. He shouldn't have come to the Rolling H, although he had turned over his scheme time and again in his mind on the ride. He sat and stared at the front porch and then jumped when he saw Charles Holcroft come out.

"Mr. Allen, that you? Come on over." The Rolling H owner motioned for him to join him. John knew the die was cast. He had to carry through with his cockeyed scheme or be a loser forever.

"I reckon you've heard the news about Mr. Kincaid," John said. He was always amazed how fast news traveled on the frontier.

"A tinker passing by early this morning told me," Holcroft said. "I'm sorry. Warner was a good man."

"You heard about his will?"

"Ah, that I did not. Is it of any interest to me?"

John almost balked again, then saw Lisa coming out of the house. The sight of her strengthened his resolve.

"It can be. Let me explain." John hurriedly outlined how Kincaid had left the ranch to his wranglers—and how quit claims from them had ended up in John's pocket.

"So you promised them double wages and took on all debt in exchange for full ownership? Amazing," Holcroft said. "What of Bill and Texas?"

"They wanted none of it, either," John said. "From their share, they're due more than the others who were mostly just hired a few months back."

"Rancher Allen," Holcroft said, laughing. "An audacious move on your part."

"You know how far in debt Mr. Kincaid was, don't you, sir? You offered to buy the Flying K from him before he died."

"That's true." The laughter lines around Holcroft's eyes hardened. "Am I correct in believing you gathered all the quit claims to the Flying K so you could offer it to me, turn a fast profit and move on?"

"No, sir!" John didn't try to hide his outrage. "I know exactly how much money is owed the creditors."

"I am not a banker and have no desire to be one. If Jack Burlison at Rancher's Bank won't loan you the money, I won't go even one cent."

"Papa, really. Mr. Allen is only asking—" Lisa was silenced by her father's cold glare.

"I could never ask for a loan, sir."

"What is it you're asking for? I don't understand."

"I figure the five hundred acres adjoining your spread is worth more than fifteen hundred dollars."

"What? That land? Ridiculous. It's not worth half that much."

"It gives access to the river. You could fatten your cattle on the land after roundup and have enough water for a herd half again the size you're running now. More cattle mean more profits," John said.

"True, but the land is hardly worth that princely sum."

Holcroft and John dickered for more than an hour before shaking hands. When they concluded their business, John had adequate money to cover current expenses and pay off the most vocal of the Flying K creditors. Selling half the Flying K's best land was a desperate measure but the only way he could retain even a part of the spread.

"You drive a hard bargain, sir. It's been ages since I felt this good." Holcraft signed his name to the bank draft with a flourish and handed the check to John.

"Neither of us won outright, sir," John said. "We both win a little."

Holcroft eyed him and let the smile slowly return to his lips. "I'll be willing to sell back the land at the end of the season."

"Oh? For how much?"

"Two thousand is a decent price for such fine property," Holcroft said.

"For land you just paid only half that for? Well, sir, we can dicker over that when I've delivered the herd to the Cheyenne railhead."

"I look forward to it, Mr. Allen. And I must say, you've worn me out. Lisa, will you help me back inside? I need to find the survey for the ranch and redraw the boundaries to include five hundred new acres."

Lisa started to say something to John, then simply winked broadly at him before going inside with her father.

John heaved a sigh and stared at the check in his hand. He had cut off half Kincaid's ranch but he had saved it— for the moment. He had to get the herd to market and sell it at a decent price to stay afloat. But already he thought on ways of buying back the land and perhaps making an offer for a few adjoining acres the Rolling H would never use but which would enhance Flying K grazing.

He went to find Arroyo but the horse had vanished. John tried to remember if he had tied down the reins and couldn't. He had been too nervous facing Holcroft to be certain what he had done. Walking out toward the barn and its watering troughs, John saw Arroyo chewing on a mouthful of hay found somewhere.

"There you are," he said, patting the strawberry on the face. "I thought I'd lost you."

"Doesn't matter much what happens to your horse," came a cold voice. "You won't be needin' it, except to drag your coffin to the cemetery."

John turned and saw Whitey Yarbrough standing, legs wide and hand hovering over the butt of his six-shooter.

"I'm not armed."

"I'm going to lose a night or two of sleep over shooting you down, then, you meddling fool. Why'd you have to go pokin' around and find out about my gambling?"

"No debt," John said. "You aren't good at gambling but there's no debt. Where did the money come from?"

"You know where it came from," Yarbrough growled. "You know I'm responsible for all the rustling."

"The Square 7 is your brand?"

"The best running brand I ever thought up," the man confirmed. "I could have stolen cattle for another year if it hadn't been for you."

"Why? You'll own the Rolling H one day." John stared

at the man and saw how anxious Yarbrough was to draw and fire. If he kept him talking he prolonged his life, for whatever good that did. John knew death stared at him straight on.

"I don't want to marry her. It's more profitable letting someone else pay the bills and leave me nothing but the profits. I'm just sorry I didn't get a second shot at the old man when I had the chance."

"You shot Mr. Holcroft?" This shook John almost as much as learning of Kincaid's death.

"Of course I did. He almost caught us rustling that night." Yarbrough pushed his coat out of the way as he prepared to draw. "I have business to attend to now. Prepare to swallow some lead." Yarbrough's hand opened and closed reflexively, then he placed his palm against the holster as he readied to draw.

"If you want to use that hogleg, Yarbrough, you'd better think on aiming it in my direction." Carver Norton moved at the edge of John's vision, coming over from the corral. "I saw Arroyo and wondered what was happening. Glad I did. I heard enough to put your neck in a noose, Yarbrough."

"So I need to kill two of you!" Even as he spoke, Yarbrough was slapping leather.

Both men's hands flashed to their six-guns—and Yarbrough was a split second faster. His bullet caught Norton in the shoulder, sending him reeling. The wrangler's six-shooter dropped to the ground and lay shining in the sun.

"Carver!" John rushed to the man and knelt. Carver had taken the bullet in the shoulder and lay shaking, color drained from his face.

"Get out of here, John. Save yourself," Carver said in a hoarse whisper. "He's too good with that iron, and he's a killer. I heard what he did." Carver's eyelids fluttered and then he sagged in John's arms.

John turned and looked around desperately. Carver's gun lay a few feet away. His eyes darted from the six-shooter to Yarbrough, who grinned wickedly. The six-shooter in his hand still smoked from the deadly shot. The world spun around John Allen in a crazy kaleidoscope that refused to slow down.

"Pick it up. I won't have murder on my conscience if you make it a fair fight."

John bent over, took up the six-shooter, hefted it, then thrust it into his belt. He stood and squared his shoulders, staring steadily at Yarbrough.

"Sam told me how you are about six-shooters. This is going to be fun," the rustler said.

"One question," John called. "Is your brother involved in the rustling too?"

"Sam's got nothing to do with it. It's all my doing, me and about half the wranglers on the Rolling H. The only thing he ever did wrong was to fall in love with the marshal's daughter. The danged fool."

"Wait. One more question. Do you love Lisa Holcroft?"

"Love her?" The laughter gave John his answer. He felt a curious mixture of outrage, vindication and relief.

Yarbrough went for his six-shooter. John's hand moved faster. He had Carver's six-gun out and got off a shot before Yarbrough cleared leather. Yarbrough started numbly at his chest where a red flower blossomed. His eyes lifted to John and the smoking gun in his hand. He started to say something, then sank down as if all the bones in his legs had turned to jelly.

Chapter Seventeen

"John!"

John Allen lowered the six-shooter and turned toward Lisa Holcroft and her father. The elder Holcroft held a shotgun in his hands pointed directly at him. John saw how the ranch owner's knuckle had turned white with the pressure on the double triggers. The slightest tug would send two barrels of buckshot right into him.

For a moment they stood frozen, then Holcroft lowered the shotgun when he saw that the gunfire was over and that the six-shooter hung limply in John's fingers. The man's hand shook, and he was visibly relieved that the deadly exchange had ended.

"He killed Whitey," Lisa said. She knelt beside the slain foreman. His glistening blood dotted her fingertips.

"He shot Carver," John said. "And he's behind the rustling. He—"

"Shut your mouth," Holcroft said harshly. "You don't speak ill of the dead, especially when you're the one who killed him."

"If I hadn't, he would have killed me, like he did Carver. Carver heard him confess and—"

"I said to be quiet," Holcroft repeated, lifting the shotgun again and training it on John. "See how Mr. Norton is faring."

Lisa knelt beside Carver and pressed her fingertips into his throat. She left bloody spots where she touched—the blood came from the man who had killed Carver.

John's eyes widened when he saw Carver kick feebly and the eyelids flutter again.

"Don't strain, Mr. Norton," Lisa said. "We'll get you into town so the doctor can patch you up." She looked at John, her eyes flashing. "Did he shoot you? Did John Allen gun you down?"

Carver rolled his head from side to side and tried to speak, but no words came out.

"He's trying to tell you," John said frantically. "I didn't shoot him. I killed Whitey, but it was in self defense. Check his six-gun. It's been fired. Whitey put the slug into Carver."

"There's more going on here than I can figure out," Holcroft said. "Lisa, bring the wagon around. We'll get Mr. Norton to town forthwith so we can hear his version of this . . . massacre."

"Give me that." Lisa yanked the six-gun from John's numbed fingers. She handed it to her pa, then lifted her skirts and rushed off to fetch the wagon.

"What I said is true, Mr. Holcroft." Words came easier with Lisa gone, but not by much. "Whitey is behind the rustling. Some of your cowboys are in it with him. Carver overheard before he was going to shoot me and—"

"I'll make sure you're good and quiet if I have to ask you to shut your tater trap one more time." Holcroft tucked the shotgun under his arm and held the six-gun Lisa had taken.

John stood mutely, trying to focus his thoughts and failing completely. How could he make them see everything he said was true? All they had seen was a smoking gun in his hand, their dead foreman and Carver in a bad way on the ground. Who should they believe?

After all, Lisa was betrothed to Yarbrough and the man her father had just entered a land deal with stood over him with a smoking gun in his hand.

Not knowing what else to do, John knelt beside his wounded friend and pulled back Carver's bloodstained red-and–black-checked shirt. Yarbrough's bullet had driven smack dab in the middle of Carver's right shoulder and had gone completely through, tearing out a hunk of flesh from his back. The wound was already clotting over, so Carver wasn't losing any more blood. That didn't mean he was not in a bad way.

"We'll get you into town. It's going to be all right.

You're not going to get out of riding herd this easy," John said. The humor was forced, but Carver's eyes were fixed on him now and a slight smile crept onto the man's lips.

Rattling of chains and creaking of wood pulled him away from Carver. Lisa stood in the driver's box and put her foot onto the brake, bringing the wagon to a halt. She jumped down but her father held her back, pressing the six-shooter into her hands.

"Watch him like a hawk," Holcroft said, "while we get Carver into the wagon."

John didn't have to be told that Lisa might shoot him outright. He had just gunned down her husband-to-be. She thought he had committed murder, so killing him would only be justice. Forcing that from his mind, he got his hands under Carver's shoulders while Holcroft grabbed the man's feet. They heaved him into the wagon bed onto a pile of empty burlap sacks.

"The bullet went clean through so there's no need to dig it out," John said. "He's not got any pink froth on his lips, so the bullet missed his lung. I should—"

"You drive," Holcroft said, swinging the shotgun around again. "Keep a steady pace and don't leave the road. We'll tend Mr. Norton."

"I've got some water, Papa," Lisa said. "He'll need it."

John climbed into the driver's box, checked to be sure his passengers were ready, then got the team pulling. He wasn't experienced with a double team and found himself straining more than he should have, but the exertion and need for constant attention kept him from thinking too much about what was likely to happen when they reached Chugwater.

It didn't look good for him. Not good at all.

A few times he cast a quick glance over his shoulder to see how Carver fared. Lisa held his head in her lap to cushion the jolts as the wagon hit one pothole after another. A couple of times John saw her dribbling water onto Carver's lips while Holcroft bent low to put his ear closer. He wanted to call out to Carver, to beg him to tell what had happened, but he held his tongue.

Eventually they rattled into Chugwater. John drove directly for the doctor's office. Holcroft shouted as they went to alert everyone of the trouble, and a few urchins ran ahead to be sure the doctor was ready when they arrived.

"You surely do get the most shot-up cowboys of any rancher in these parts," the doctor said to Holcroft as four men slid Carver from the wagon.

"Is he going to be all right?" John called. He kept his hands on the reins because Lisa pointed the six-shooter directly at him. And her hands did not shake. Her aim would be deadly if she opened fire at this close range.

Somehow, all that mattered to him now was Carver. He brightened when he saw Carver struggling to stand. One man had to support him, but the cowboy was strong enough to take a couple shaky steps in his direction.

"John, John," Carver said, fighting to get the words out. "You don't know how to use a six-shooter. But I've never seen a man faster or luckier."

"Lucky? There wasn't any luck to it."

He was surprised when Lisa silently handed him the six-shooter she had trained on him seconds earlier.

"Reckon I'm from Missouri," Carver said. "Show me."

John swung the six-shooter around and fired four times. Each of the bullets crashed into a post holding up an awning over the doctor's doorway, spaced so tightly that a dime could cover the tight pattern. "I'm more inclined to rely on skill than luck."

"When did you learn to shoot like that? Did Bill Diamond—"

"I learned when I was an apprentice gunsmith. Yarbrough made the same mistake you did, Carver. Just because I don't cotton to wearing a six-gun doesn't mean I can't use one." He handed the empty pistol back to Carver. "Thanks for the loan."

"You should keep it. You used it better'n I did," Carver said. His strength fled and the man beside him had to grab to keep him from falling.

"Get him inside. I declare, if you people aren't shooting each other, you're talking your ears off," grumbled the doctor. John let out a deep sigh. Carver was going to be all right. He felt it in his gut.

John looked over at Lisa. Her blue eyes bored into him. Tears welled and threatened to run down her cheeks.

"Carver told you, didn't he? On the way here. He told you what Yarbrough said about you and him?" John asked. "I'm sorry. I would have spared you if—"

"Carver said he would have murdered you where you stood, but you talked him into that horrible gunfight," Lisa said, tears running down her cheeks now. "I . . . I'm glad he didn't kill you. He was an awful man!"

John stood helplessly as sobs wracked the young woman. He looked at her father, who scowled at him. He motioned for John to go to Lisa. Awkwardly, he took her in his arms and held her. It felt strange at first, her crying into his shoulder. He felt hot tears on his shirt and skin. Then the awkwardness passed and it felt right holding her, comforting her, as if this was what he was meant to do.

"Get out of the sun or you'll get heat prostration," Holcroft said. "Don't wander off now, you hear? I have many things to discuss with Marshal Lane."

They sat in chairs by the door leading to the doctor's surgery, saying nothing, holding hands. John couldn't help but think of all that had happened. Whitey Yarbrough had died instantly from his accurately aimed bullet. John shuddered and closed his eyes for a moment. He had never killed a man before, but there had been no choice. Whitey was a rustler, a bushwhacker and a murderer.

He had done more than defend himself. He had saved Carver's life—and maybe Lisa Holcroft's. If Yarbrough felt no remorse at ambushing the woman's father, why stop there? He looked into Lisa's azure eyes and knew he would do it again. A million times again, if it kept her from harm.

* * *

"There are my men now, Marshal," Holcroft said from a vantage in front of the jail. He shielded his eyes against the sun as three of his cowhands led a horse with Yarbrough draped over the saddle to the side of the jail-house. "You can take possession of Yarbrough's body now. Bury him in the potter's field, for all I care."

"Yes, sir, reckon I will. Just leave the corpse draped over the horse, will you, boys?" Marshal Lane turned and looked John square in the eyes. "That all right with you, Mr. Allen?"

John's eyebrows rose when he heard the note of respect in the lawman's voice.

"We got a full statement from Mr. Holcroft and won't need much from you. He makes Whitey out to be the one responsible for the rustling. There was plenty of evidence in Whitey's belongings, and they found a running iron for the Square 7 brand. Don't know what more evidence I need. That about sum it up, Mr. Allen?"

"Just about, Marshal," John said. "I want to add that Sam Yarbrough didn't have any part of the cattle thieving. From the way Whitey talked, his brother didn't know anything, even that his older brother was responsible."

"Sam's not too bright. I can believe it of him. He's a hothead but not bad." The marshal turned to go back into the office when John stopped him. He started to make a case for Sam with the marshal's daughter, then thought better of it. Let Sam and Cara work out their problems. They'd be better for it. Instead, he asked another question that had ridden like a burr under a saddle blanket.

"What of the Square 7 cattle? Since Whitey admitted that was a run brand, it means all the cattle wearing it on their hips are stolen. How do we divide them up?"

"I suppose it might be a matter for the court, but the judge isn't likely to want to deal with it. Not when I might be bringing in more rustlers. Mr. Holcroft said half his hands were responsible for all the troubles." The marshal shook his head in disbelief. "I reckon I'm going to have to run them down. By now they'll have heard about Whitey's death and be scattering to the four winds."

"Mr. Allen, we can deal privately with the problem of the Square 7 cattle," said Holcroft. "The only beeves stolen are likely to have been either Flying K or Rolling H."

"Well, yes, that seems so, Mr. Holcroft, but we'll have to examine each cow and—"

"I have a better idea, Papa. We're going to be short quite a few hands for the drive to Cheyenne." Lisa had dried her tears, though dusty tracks remained on her cheeks. Her eyes blazed. John wasn't sure he had ever seen her looking more alive—or more beautiful.

"That's so," Holcroft admitted. "The ones that don't end up in Marshal Lane's jail will never be seen again. We might be *very* shorthanded."

"Perhaps Mr. Allen would accept all the stolen cattle in return for help from his wranglers. We could drive both herds together. In Cheyenne it would be easy enough to separate them, Rolling H from all the others."

"I know Archie Benjamin well, and he is a lodge brother. I can explain what has happened." Holcroft nodded as he spoke. He glanced up at John, saw his puzzled look and explained. "Archie is the buying agent for the Chicago slaughterhouses. He is a stickler when it comes to brands and would never allow two different brands to be tallied against a single account. This is a unique situation, however."

"Most of the cattle Yarbrough stole would be from the Rolling H," John said. "Are you sure you wish to make such a generous offer?"

"Of course I am. Lisa's got a good head on her shoulders. The Rolling H will be coming out ahead. We have a *lot* of cattle, and it will not be a simple task moving so many, not when you have your own beeves to deal with."

"My cowpunchers are pulling double wages. They ought to earn them," John said, filling with pride as he spoke.

His wranglers.

Realizing he had other business in town, John bid Holcroft and his daughter good-bye and turned toward the far end of Chugwater and the Ranchers Bank. He had a check from Mr. Holcroft to present to the bank president. That thousand dollars would go a long ways toward seeing debts paid and the herd driven to the railhead.

As he walked down the street, he couldn't keep from whistling a jaunty tune. Never had the sun seemed warmer nor the day finer.

Epilogue

"That's about the best drive I've ever been part of," Carver Norton said with great gusto. "Let me buy you a drink, John."

"He doesn't drink," Texas Dunn cut in. "That makes celebratin' with him real cheap, but you can buy me one."

"Watch out, Carver," John said. "It might be cheap since I don't drink, but Texas is a bottomless well. What you save with me, you're bound to lose with him."

"Quit your complaining, the lot of you. With the bonus riding in my pocket, I can afford to buy everyone drinks," Bill Diamond called out. "To John Allen. The best boss any wrangler could have!"

A cheer went up in the saloon. John accepted a mug of cider and sipped at it tentatively, then drank more deeply when he made sure it wasn't hard cider. Some vices he would never start, and drinking hard liquor was one.

Wearing a six-shooter was another. He saw no reason. Bill wore his and so did Carver. But most of the men riding with them down to Cheyenne City had not been weighed down by three pounds of iron at their hip and they had arrived just fine with both herds. They had spent the summer fattening the cattle in pastures and with hay specially baled for the purpose, and the drive from Chugwater to Cheyenne had lasted only twelve days.

The Rolling H stock had been quickly separated and Charles Holcroft had gone off to negotiate his price. Taking the Square 7 beeves as his due for helping get the other rancher's herd to market, John had a sizable herd of his own to sell for the Flying K. Warner Kincaid would have been proud of the price garnered for the beeves, and he would have popped his buttons knowing every man on his spread received double wages *and* a sizable bonus.

John knew a little of that success had to be attributed to Holcroft. The rancher had done his level best to get John a good price with the slaughterhouse agent. But enough of the high price had come from John's own ability to argue and negotiate and come to terms on his own. He had come up against a slick dealer in Archie Benjamin and had held his own.

Now, back in Chugwater on his way to the Flying K, he felt at ends. John could hardly believe the ranch house was his—as was the entire spread. Or what remained of it after selling five hundred acres to Mr. Holcroft.

"You have enough seed money to start on next year's general roundup?" Carver asked. "You got to see to the bulls, make sure the cows are ready for 'em, then tend the calves. Veterinary supplies don't come cheap. And you will want some breeding stock. A new bull or two would go a ways toward a decent herd."

"You worry too much," John said. "You might be my top hand, but you ought to let the foreman chew me out." He glanced over at Bill. The man nodded slowly.

"I do want to thank you, John. You held the wranglers together. Not a one of them doesn't want to stay on over the winter, just so they'd be around next spring when you really need 'em to get down to serious work. That's a mighty high recommendation for you."

"We all have confidence in you, boy," Texas said. "I figure it might take all winter to get you to appreciate my food, but—"

"I should live that long," John said. "Eating your food, I might not live that long!" He enjoyed the good-natured joking going on. They had done what he had thought impossible. The Flying K had turned enough of a profit to pay off the creditors and to establish a small line of credit with the Ranchers Bank.

John smiled wryly. Banker Jack Burlison had even offered to sponsor him as an apprentice in the lodge. Things were looking up. But the money was burning a hole in his pocket.

"You're looking antsy, John. Where are you planning to go? Out to the ranch?"

"Not yet. It's not home. Not my home," he tried to explain. "First, I want to finish some business I started with Mr. Holcroft."

"And what might that be?" Carver inquired. "Something to do with the land you sold off?"

"No."

"Let me guess," Bill cut in, trying hard to hide his broad grin and failing. "You want to be sure no more of those Square 7 cattle are eating up the rangeland."

"No."

"He's got something more on his mind, gents," Texas declared. "But what could it be? What could a drifter like John Allen be thinking about?"

John flushed. They knew him too well.

"You got it wrong on one score, Texas," John said. "I don't reckon I'm a drifter anymore."

He'd go out to the Rolling H and dicker a mite about the land. Just to break the ice. Then he would change the subject around to asking for Lisa's hand in marriage. They had gotten to know each other well over the summer, and he saw no reason Holcroft wouldn't be agreeable to a wedding since his daughter already was.

And if he didn't consent, why, he'd just have to be persuaded. John could be mighty persuasive when he put his mind to it, and the woman he loved was the reward.